"Rocket-boosted action, brilliant speculation, and the recreation of a horror out of the mythologic past, all seamlessly blend into a rollercoaster ride of suspense and adventure."
-- James Rollins, New York Times bestselling author of JAKE RANSOM AND THE SKULL KING'S SHADOW

"With THRESHOLD Jeremy Robinson goes pedal to the metal into very dark territory. Fast-paced, action-packed and wonderfully creepy! Highly recommended!"
--Jonathan Maberry, NY Times bestselling author of ROT & RUIN

"Jeremy Robinson is the next James Rollins"
-- Chris Kuzneski, NY Times bestselling author of THE SECRET CROWN

"If you like thrillers original, unpredictable and chock-full of action, you are going to love Jeremy Robinson..."
-- Stephen Coonts, NY Times bestselling author of DEEP BLACK: ARCTIC GOLD

"How do you find an original story idea in the crowded action-thriller genre? Two words: Jeremy Robinson."
-- Scott Sigler, NY Times Bestselling author of ANCESTOR

"There's nothing timid about Robinson as he drops his readers off the cliff without a parachute and somehow manages to catch us an inch or two from doom."
-- Jeff Long, New York Times bestselling author of THE DESCENT

THE LAST HUNTER

DESCENT

JEREMY ROBINSON

BREAKNECK MEDIA

For the real Solomon, my son and inspiration

Visit Jeremy Robinson on the World Wide Web at:
www.jeremyrobinsononline.com

THE LAST HUNTER

Prologue
1911

Douglas Mawson tasted blood. The chapped skin of his lower lip peeled up like flakes of shaved coconut. The cold had started the injury, and then it worsened thanks to his habit of chewing the skin from his lip. But he was careful about it, nibbling at the still dying flesh like a preening bird. It was the sneeze that split the lip, tearing it down the middle. The sting cleared his mind, but the blood made him hungry. He looked around, hoping to see something that might take his mind off food, but he saw only white ice and blue sky.

Three hundred fifteen miles separated Mawson and his two men from camp; three thousand more from civilization. No man had ever ventured further from home, and only one of them would make it back.

Mawson, commander of the expedition, stood before a white glacial expanse. His angular face, typically clean-shaven but now covered by an inch-thick beard, hid behind a dirty tan scarf. The scarf did little to protect him against the Antarctic cold, which grated his lungs. The rest of him, bundled in a thick, beige snow-suit, felt warmer when moving. Not so much when standing still.

Dr. Xavier Mertz had stopped. He was the point man, riding on skis while Mawson followed with a dog sledge team and Lieu-tenant Ninnis brought up the rear with a second team and the majority of their indispensable supplies. That Mertz had stopped meant he'd seen something. Most likely something dangerous, like a snow-covered crevasse. They looked solid enough until you put weight on them. Then they could fall through like a trap door.

"What's the problem, Mertz?" Mawson shouted.

But the man didn't reply.

Mawson removed his hood in case the man's words were being muffled. He asked again, "What is it, Mertz?"

The only sign that Mertz had not frozen solid on the spot was his head, craning slowly from side to side.

Mawson signaled for Ninnis to remain behind and stepped off his sledge. He petted the nearest dog as he passed, then headed for Mertz. His feet crunched over the snow and ice, signaling his approach. Still, the man did not move.

Five feet away, Mertz finally responded, his hand snapping up with an open palm. The sudden movement sent Mawson's heart pounding. But the message was clear: *Don't. Move.* And he didn't. Not for three minutes. Then he spoke again. "Bloody hell, Mertz, what is it?"

Mertz turned his head slightly. "Saw someone."

"Saw something?"

"Some-*one*."

Ridiculous, Mawson thought. They were the first human beings to set foot in this part of the world. So sure was he of that fact that he spoke his mind aloud. "Ridiculous."

He stepped up to Mertz's side. "The land is frozen. Not only is there no way a man could live here, there's nowhere to hide."

Mertz turned to Mawson. "He wasn't wearing clothes."

Mawson frowned. Mertz had a reputation for being a humorous fellow. "My lip is split. My knees are sore. My stomach is rumbling. I'm not in the mood for jokes, so let's go. I want to be off this glacier before dark."

"His hair was red. As red as the blood staining your beard. But his body was pale." Mertz returned his eyes to the snow. "Wouldn't have seen him if not for the hair."

Mawson's patience wore thin. "Mertz," he growled more than said.

The man turned to him and Mawson saw wide-eyed fear. "I'm *not* joking."

With his eyes shut, Mawson took a deep breath. The energy he'd exert losing his temper would drain him later on. He'd need that strength to survive. Calming his voice, he said, "Mertz, look around. What do you see?"

He glanced at Mertz, who was indeed looking. "White. From horizon to horizon. White! There is no one there. Not now. Not before. And if we stand here one more minute, we will—"

A sound like a howl rolled across the frozen plain. Mawson's voice caught in his throat. It sounded...human. But it wasn't. "The wind," he said quickly, noticing the deepening wrinkles on

Mertz's sunburned forehead.

Why hadn't the man covered his skin? Mawson thought. Before he could ask, a second, louder howl echoed around them.

Before Mawson could once again dismiss the sound, Mertz spoke. "There's not a breeze to speak of."

Mawson held his breath. Mertz was right.

Mertz looked at him again. *I told you so*, his expression said. But as he turned away, his head spun back around, past Mawson, toward Ninnis. His eyes popped wide. His arm reached out. A high pitched, "No!" shot from his mouth.

Mawson turned around in time to see the last of the sledge dogs pulled toward a hole in the ice. It whimpered, digging its claws into the ice. Then it was gone. Ninnis, six dogs and the sledge had disappeared. The glacier had come to life and swallowed them whole.

The two men ran for the spot where Ninnis had been. They stopped short, sliding on their feet as the ice opened up before them. Ninnis had parked the sledge atop a crevasse. Had they but continued moving, he would have made it across.

Mawson lay on his stomach, dispersing his weight, and slid to the mouth of the gaping hole. One hundred and fifty feet below, on a ledge, lay a lone dog. It twitched between whimpers, its spine broken. Ninnis and the other five dogs were gone, disappeared into the darkness beyond.

"Ninnis!" Mawson shouted. "Ninnis! Lieutenant! Can you hear me? Are you alive, man?"

There was no reply. He suspected there never would be. But they couldn't just leave him. For three hours the two men shouted until their voices grew hoarse. They tied all their ropes together, but the line wasn't even long enough to reach the now dead sledge dog.

Distraught over the loss of their colleague and friend, Mawson and Mertz didn't want to give up hope. But they had no choice. Ninnis had fallen with most of their food, their tents and warm weather gear. To survive the three hundred fifteen mile journey back to base camp, they couldn't spend one more minute mourning the man.

Mawson peeled a frozen tear from his cheek and returned to his sledge. They needed to move.

As they maneuvered the remaining sledge, and dogs, which would later become their food, around the crevasse, neither man heard the muffled cries coming from below. They left without pause, on a journey that would claim the lives of all six dogs and Mertz. Mawson alone would survive the journey and eventually return home to England.

But Ninnis would outlive them both.

Had either man thought to descend the rope they'd fashioned, they would have found their man tucked inside a hollow hidden by an overhang only fifty feet from the surface. After regaining consciousness, he'd tried to call out to them, to reach for the rope, but some unseen force pinned him down. An hour after Mawson and Mertz gave up the search, a hand so white it was nearly translucent, came away from his mouth.

"Welcome home, Ninnis," a voice whispered in his ear, the breath smelling like rotten, jellied eel.

Ninnis filled his lungs and let out a scream, but the sound was cut short as he was taken by his collar and dragged deeper into the ice.

1

I scream.

    I'm too terrified to do anything else. My hands are on my head. I'm pitched forward. My eyes are clenched shut. Every muscle in my body has gone tight, as though clutched in rigor.

    The monster knocks me back and I spill into a pile of bones and old skin. But I feel no weight on top of me. No gnashing of teeth on my body. The thing has missed its tackle, striking a glancing blow as it passed, but nothing more. Perhaps because I bent down. Perhaps because it can't see well in the dark. I don't know. I don't care.

    I'm alive. For now.

    And I don't want to die.

    But I'm certain I'm going to and the events of the past few months replay in my mind. I can't stop it. I can't control it. And in a flash, I'm back at the beginning.

I've been told that the entire continent of Antarctica groaned at the moment of my birth. The howl tore across glaciers, over mountains and deep into the ice. Everyone says so. Except for my father; all he heard was Mother's sobs. Not of pain, but of joy, so he says. Other than that, the only verifiable fact about the day I was born is that an iceberg the size of Los Angeles broke free from the ice shelf a few miles off the coast. Again, some would have me believe the fracture took place as I entered the world. But all that really matters, according to my parents, is that I, Solomon Ull Vincent, the first child born on Antarctica—the first and only Antarctican—was born on September 2nd, 1974, thirteen years ago, today.

Of course, I don't buy my parents' seeming lack of memory when it comes to my birth. When I broach the topic they start ducking and weaving like spastic boxers. What I'm sure of is that something strange occurred when I was born; something that frightened them enough to bury all record of it. And they've done a good job. I've searched in and behind every drawer in this house. I've scoured the attic and the basement. I've even flipped through every one of the thousands of books they have on shelves around the house in search of a hollowed-out core. I've found nothing. But occasionally, at a Christmas party or get together, someone who heard the story slips up and reveals a tidbit before covering their mouth and offering an, "Oops."

They think they're protecting me, but all they're really doing is making me feel like a freak. More of a freak, I should say. Every one else I come into contact with thinks I'm weird, too. My parents just feign ignorance.

In celebration of my uncommon birth, my family is celebrating in the most common way imaginable: a quiet dinner at home. In attendance are my parents, Mark and Beth, and my only real friend, Justin McCarthy. We eat in silence, first enjoying the hot orange grease of Maria's Pizza, and then the fudgy, chunky center of a Dairy Queen ice-cream cake, all polished off by tall glasses of Cherry Coke.

Nothing like massive amounts of fat and sugar to make you feel older.

Though the party, if you can call it that, is a subdued affair, I look at the gifts with great anticipation, the way a lion does a zebra before pouncing—hunter's eyes. I don't want toys. Didn't ask for any. Not interested, despite grandfather's continuous donations of G.I. Joes. My parents always know what to get me. Because despite their constant lies about my past, they're like me.

Smart. Uncommonly so.

Nerds. Geeks. Bookworms. I'd heard all the names at school. Being smarter than everyone in my class exacerbated the issue. No senior in high school likes to be upstaged or outsmarted by a thirteen-year-old with a cracking voice. Though I sometimes wonder if their real problem with me was my resistance to 1980's pop-culture; I don't feather my hair, wear friendship bracelets, or watch Music Television. It doesn't matter now. All that went away when my parents decided to home-school me. My nervousness, tension and boredom has been replaced by excitement, learning and stimulation. Not to mention a name-calling cease fire.

Well, almost. My parents call me Schwartz. The name evolved from my mother's first nickname for me: first and only, which was short for the "first and only baby born on Antarctica." They quickly shortened it to FAO and then, thanks to the FAO Schwartz department store, I became Schwartz. After the movie *Spaceballs* came out a few months ago, my parents stopped using the name in front of Justin because, almost as a Pavlovian response, Justin would say, "I see your Schwartz is as big as mine."

The first gifts I open are books—fiction and non-fiction, popular and obscure—I like them all. Next come three boxes of Robotix kits. I'll put the dinosaur-looking robot on the cover to shame with the creature I'll create. The biggest box comes last. I tear into the bright blue wrapping paper as Justin slurps grease from a leftover pizza slice.

The loud slurp stops short and grease drips on to Justin's plate. "Whoa," he says.

To Justin, this is a "whoa" moment. He likes to blow things up. To me it's a big letdown. My parents see my down-turned lips even as I fight to reverse them.

"You have to build it yourself," mom says.

"The box says it mimics the pattern of a real lava flow," dad adds.

I let out a grunt, wondering if my parents IQs have dropped. Or maybe they've finally given up caring? The gift is nothing more than a cardboard cone, some quick drying clay, a pouch of red-colored baking soda and a small bottle of vinegar. This is the *big present?* They had gone on about how surprised I would be. About how incredible the gift was. This is...simple.

Boring.

Justin punches my shoulder. It hurts. I know he didn't mean it to, but I seem to feel pain more than other people. Justin's dark brown eyes are impossible to see behind the tinted sports glasses he always wears, but I know they're wide with excitement. I focus on that to avoid thinking about the pain in my arm.

"Are there any G.I. Joes we haven't melted?" he asks.

"A few."

"Let's go!" Justin dashes from the dining room and takes the stairs two at a time. "C'mon!" he shouts from the top.

"Go ahead," mom says. "He has to go home in an hour. Mass starts at six in the morning."

Saturday morning mass is something I never understood. It's a sacred time. Not mass, mind you. Saturday mornings. A bowl of Cocoa Pebbles starts the morning. *Starvengers, Gaiking, Robotech* and more, followed by Creature Double Feature, which promises at least one *Godzilla* movie, fills my day until noon. It is a TV line-up so good that I am sure God skips mass for it too.

"May I be excused?" I ask with a sigh.

Dad chuckles. It's the kind of chuckle that's a substitute for calling someone stupid. I've heard the laugh enough to recognize the sound. "You don't need to ask after we told you to go."

I brush some of my long blond hair, which has garnered more than a few Einstein taunts, out of my face. Mom and Dad wear unreadable smiles. Like they know something I don't. I hate that feeling—I've felt it every day of my life—so I slide off the chair, pick up the large, but light, volcano box and march it upstairs. When I hear mother giggle—just like the kids at school used to— a tear forms in my eye.

I'm such a wimp. No, wimp isn't the word. That's like calling someone a chicken. Means they're afraid to fight—which also describes me—but that isn't what I mean. *Crybaby*. That's the word. One laugh from my mother and I'm all weepy. Of course, the laugh combined with the silly present confirms that they don't take me seriously. And if they don't take me seriously, they'll never notice I'm not a kid anymore—if you ignore the fact that I'm about to bury a bunch of action figures in a miniature volcano—and that means they'll never reveal the mysteries surrounding my birth. I'm not sure why the day I was born interests me so much. You don't hear other kids asking about when they were born. But there is something in me, something raw, which longs to know more.

As I near the top of the stairs I wipe my eyes dry and focus on the soft rug lining the stairs. It feels squishy beneath my socks. I find it comforting. Through the banister rungs I see Justin hunkering over a fishing lure case filled with odd toys. I scuff my feet, sliding sock against rug. I walk like that all the way to the bedroom doorway.

"Put out your hand," I say.

Justin does.

I reach out a single finger and touch it to Justin's palm. A tiny blue arch of electricity zaps between us with a sharp crack. Justin yelps and flinches away, knocking over the box of toys. "Hey!" he shouts and then moves to retaliate with a finger flick.

I put the volcano box between us and raise an eyebrow.

Justin pauses. "Ugh, fine. Oh! I almost forgot." He fishes into his pants pocket and pulls out a clear blue cassette tape. Then he closes the door. "My cousin made this for me. Said my mom wouldn't let me listen to it."

He puts the cassette into the shoebox sized tape-deck and hits play. Loud music, unlike anything I've heard before, fills the room.

I place the volcano box on the floor and let Justin tear into it. I sit down on the bed hearing the music, but not really listening. My eyes turn to the wall, where a five foot by five foot poster of Antarctica is tacked up. I've marked all the active United States bases—McMurdo, Amundsen-Scott, Palmer, Siple, Willard—as well as some of the larger foreign stations. A bright green circle marks one of the few bases that no longer functions: Clark. Snow and ice buried the site within a year of my birth. How does something like that happen? Even on Antarctica. Just another one of the mysteries no one seems to know anything about.

Though I haven't been there since shortly after my birth, I miss the place. I've become an expert on the continent and hope to return when I'm old enough. There are so many interesting aspects of Antarctica I long to explore. The founder of Clark Station, Dr. Merrill Clark, is my personal hero. His search for evidence of a human Antarctican civilization—my geographic ancestors—captivates me. And I want to follow in his footsteps.

But it will be a long time before that can happen. I doubt my parents will let me go until I'm eighteen and they can't stop me. Of course, I do understand some of the reasons I'm not yet able

to go. I might be smarter than most adults, but I'm also smart
enough to know I have the emotional fortitude of an eight year
old. Happens with smart kids, I've read. Understanding how awful the world can be is hard for someone without emotional de-
fenses. I should be more concerned with the outcome of the daily
ant battles waged on our sidewalk than the starving children in
Ethiopia. I stopped watching the news a year ago. The images
tended to fuel my imagination, which was not a good thing.

I'm painfully shy, especially around girls. I'm quick to cry, especially if someone is angry with me. And, though no one knows
it, I'm afraid of the dark. Not just afraid, I'm *terrified* of the dark.
It's not a fear of what might lurk in the shadows, closets or under
the bed. I'm afraid of my own thoughts. When my imagination is
freed from the coils of intentional thought, it drifts to places far
darker than deepest black. The horrors of school, of starving kids
on TV, and of my parents' mortality are passing thoughts by
comparison.

I sometimes wonder if the dark thoughts are a true reflection
of what lies within. Of my soul.

The words of the music finally sink in. "What's a brick
house?" I ask.

Justin shrugs as he places a volcano-shaped cardboard cone
onto a sheet of plastic.

"Thirty six, twenty four, thirty six. Are those measurements? Is
this a song about construction? Why wouldn't your moth—"

"They're measurements all right," my friend says with a fien-
dish grin, then holds his hands in front of his chest like he's gripping two baseballs. "For boobs."

My immediate embarrassment is multiplied tenfold when I hear mother clear her throat. I spin toward the door, mortified.

"Forty-five minutes," she says with a grimace. She closes the door behind her as she leaves.

"Thanks a lot," putting as much anger into my whisper as I can manage.

Justin, who is unfazed by these events, tugs open the pre-moistened bag of quick drying clay. "Just for the record, your mom is a brick house."

I rub my socks on the rug.

"Ok, ok!" Justin says. "Just help me put this together. We have forty-five minutes to blow it up."

I sit down next to him and look at the materials. There's enough here to make three mediocre eruptions. All for—I look at the box—thirty bucks. There has to be a way to make sure my parents get their money's worth out of this thing. I smile as the idea comes to me.

* * *

We finish forty minutes later. The quick dry clay is solid and authentic looking if you ignore the embedded action figures. *Nice knowing you, Snake Eyes.* But there are a few invisible modifications. First we expanded the internal cylinder that holds the red-dyed baking soda. Instead of three small eruptions, we will now have one large one. And to make things really exciting, we sealed the top of the volcano. This eruption will be as genuine as I can make it.

We both hold syringes pilfered from a chemistry set. Each contains six ounces of vinegar. "On the count of three," I say. "One."

"Is this going to explode?" Justin asks.

"Two."

"Should we wear safety goggles?" He grins before touching his sports glasses. "Oh wait."

"Three!"

We plunge the needles into the volcano and inject the vinegar.

The bedroom door opens. "Ok, boys. Time to—"

"Mom, get back!" I shout. But a loud hiss behind me signifies it's too late. I turn around in time to see the entire volcano, which neither I nor Justin had thought to attach to something solid, erupt—from beneath. The entire cone launches off the floor, spraying red-dyed lava as it spins in the air like one of DaVinci's airships. The cone tilts, shoots forward, slams into the poster of Antarctica, and explodes. Red gore splashes against the poster and the wall. It reminds me of the *Greatest American Hero* episode where the voodoo loving villain splatters chicken blood on the walls.

I turn to my mother. Her white blouse is covered in red streaks. There is no humor in her eyes as she looks at Justin and says, "Your mother is on her way," and then leaves.

"What happened to you?" I hear my father ask. He pokes his head in a moment later, eyes wide behind his glasses. "Oh...geez."

"Sorry," I say, eyes on the floor.

When he doesn't reply, I look up.

He's trying to mask a smile, but failing miserably. "You're lucky it's your birthday, Sol."

"How angry do you think she is?"

"Chernobyl, at least."

Chernobyl is bad, but nowhere near as bad as super nova. If dad is right, she'll be over it by morning. I smile back at my father. "It flew."

My father snickers, looking at the red stained wall. He rubs a hand through his curly black hair. "I can see that."

The doorbell rings. "That'd be your mom," Dad says to Justin before leading him from the room. He stops at the top of the stairs and turns back to me. "Clean yourself up and brush your teeth."

"What about the room?" I ask.

"No amount of scrubbing is going to get that dye out of things. We'll worry about it in the morning." He takes one step down and pauses. "Sorry about the poster, Schwartz."

I hear Justin say a quick, "I see your Schwartz is as big as mine," from the foyer before opening the front door for his mother.

I look up at the poster. The circle around my birthplace is smudged, the ink running. "Yeah..."

As my mother changes and my father explains the red dye on Justin's clothes to his mother, I enter the bathroom. Head lowered, I wash my hands and face. With water dripping from both, I reach out and take hold of a hand towel and dry myself. With the towel still over my face, I sigh. I think about my gifts. My birthday. My age. My life in general.

I sigh again. *At least tomorrow is Saturday.*

I pull the towel from my face and look in the mirror. My skin is white, like snow. My eyes are bright blue. My hair is so blond it only contains a hint of yellow. But I've seen all this before and it doesn't hold my attention. That's when I see it. Something taped to the shower door behind me. An envelope. On it, the words, "Happy Birthday", have been written backwards so I can read them in the mirror.

The envelope is in my hand a moment later. I tear into it. My eyes catch sight of what's inside. I stumble back, sitting on the toilet. As I take out the contents of the envelope, my eyes blur over. I can't read the words, but I know what I hold. Plane tickets. An itinerary. A map that looks just like the ruined poster on my wall.

"Happy birthday," the voice of my mother says. I blink my eyes. She's crouching in front of me, dressed in jeans and a gray Phil Collins T-shirt. She's smiling.

I wrap my arms around her in a burst of emotion and say, "Thank you."

My father is standing in the bathroom door. I launch at him, hugging him around the neck, feet dangling above the floor.

When he puts me down, I sniff and wipe my eyes, feeling no embarrassment over the tears. "When are we going?"

"Summer in Antarctica begins in about seven weeks."

The tears well again, as a single thought repeats in my head. *I'm going home.*

2

I can't sleep. Like the owl that hunts at night, I've gone nocturnal. My imagination is in overdrive—Justin would say, "It's gone plaid." But it's actually an improvement. I normally lose sleep to thoughts of awful things. Those frightening images don't have a chance to manifest tonight. My mind is on Antarctica. What will I see? Penguins? Weddell seals? *The South Pole*? Where will we go? Can I explore? Who will I meet?

It suddenly occurs to me that Merrill Clark himself might be there. My father has kept in loose contact with him since I was born. They worked together at Clark Station for three summers in a row. I've heard my mother tease Dad about Dr. Clark being my real father. She says the same thing about the mailman sometimes, too. So I know she's teasing. But it implies they're close. Or were. Of course, it also implies they're close to the mailman, which makes no sense, because our mailman is a mailwoman.

I also know that Dr. Clark is married. His wife's name is Aimee. She's black, which I've heard my parents talk about, too. Apparently it's taboo for people of different skin colors to marry. And they have a daughter, Mirabelle. She's a year younger than me.

Remembering the daughter makes me nervous. My parents stopped going to Antarctica after I was born. Said it wasn't a safe place to raise a baby. Maybe Dr. Clark did the same. I know he's continued publishing about Antarctica, but it could all be based on old research. I make a mental note to ask in morning. I roll over and squint. It's *already* morning. The rising sun cuts through the crack in my shade and strikes my eyes.

The nice thing about being home-schooled—at least the way my parents do it—is that I pick the subjects. I pick where, when and how I want to learn. Not only do my parents trust that I'll get a better education this way, they feel most kids would too. Dad calls school a "good citizen factory."

I think my parents were hippies.

But I agree with them.

The point is, I can sleep until noon if I want. And I'll get more learning done in an hour than most kids will during a full day of school. I roll over and close my eyes. They reopen a moment later.

It's Saturday.

I'm on my feet and scratching dried red lava from the clock face. It's not coming off, so I pull the shade and look at the sun's low position in the sky. It's September third and the sun is still rising early. I place the time around 6:30, slide into my slippers and head downstairs.

I skip the third and fifth steps because they squeak. I know the sound won't wake my parents, but I like to pretend I'm a ninja. Five minutes later I'm sitting on the floor, bowl of Cocoa Pebbles in hand. I sit at the long coffee table where my drawing paper and pencils wait.

I pick up the cable remote and remember when I had to get up to change the channel, rotate the top TV dial to U and the lower dial to channel fifty-six. I turn it on and there's a commercial featuring a bunch of women with puffy hairdos being asked what they would do for a Klondike Bar. Tell a secret? One of the women reveals that her husband works out in his underwear, and I think I'll never eat a Klondike Bar again. I tune out the next commercial and stuff my mouth with delicious artificially flavored chocolate cereal.

"I wouldn't do anything for a Klondike Bar," I say, spraying a few Pebbles on my art pad. "But I'd work out in *my* underwear for—"

I see something. Not on TV. In the sun room, which is separated from the living room by a large door with twelve small windows. Something inside the room moved. I swallow hard. Some of the not yet chewed, not yet mushy, cereal scratches my throat.

"Dad?" I say. He gets up early on occasion, but I hear no reply.

"Mom?" That my mother would be up this early on a Saturday is ludicrous. I usually don't see her until ten.

The TV is showing previews of the upcoming programming lineup so I know I have about thirty seconds before *Robotech* starts. I push the coffee table away, stand up and tiptoe toward the door. I'm a ninja again. Defenseless, but quiet. Of course, the TV has long ago announced my presence.

Maybe there was a burglar? I think. He could have been scared by the TV coming on and fled through a window. Or maybe he's still in there, waiting for the stupid twelve—make that thirteen-year-old—to check things out.

I think about going to the kitchen for a knife, but I don't like them. Every time I pick one up, if my mind isn't on something else, I see myself stabbing whoever else is in the room. I'm an unwilling, mental serial killer.

That's just *one* of my unmentionable dark thoughts.

Of course, if I get jumped by a thief, then jamming a knife into him would be completely justified.

With my thoughts full of spraying blood, I feel sick to my stomach. No knife. Not now. Not ever.

I'm at the door anyway and have yet to be jumped. I peek through the glass and scan the small, square room. There's a couch that pulls out into a bed. It fills up most of the room when opened. And there's a small desk that gets used once a year when dad does the taxes. Nothing else. No thief.

That's when I see the living room windows behind me, reflected in the glass of the door. What if I had seen a reflection? My heart begins to pound as I realize I've made myself an easy target. I feel a tingling on my neck. Hot breath. The presence behind me feels sinister.

Evil.

I spin around with a roar that scares me. My lips are curled up. My teeth grit. My hands, both of them, are open, but tight, like I've got claws to slash someone with.

But there is no one to slash. The room is empty.

I'm still scared. Terrified actually. Despite having the dark thoughts for years, this is the first time I've seen them manifest into action. The sound that came from my mouth. The roar. It didn't sound like me. I can't sustain a cord that deep without my voice cracking like a panicked goose. Worse, I was ready to kill, to tear someone apart. Had there been someone behind me, I would have attacked. It could have been a thief, or my mom, or my dad. It wouldn't have mattered.

I would have hurt them.

If I'd gone to get the knife I might have killed them.

I look at my hands, still rigid and ready to gouge.

What kind of person am I?

A sharp clap, like two boards of wood slapping together, spins me around with a shout. The noise came from the sun room. I stand there, frozen. The rapid fire beat of my heart surges oxygen to my muscles, readying them for fight or flight. But I can see most of the sun room still. There is no one there.

The sound repeats, this time to the right, and I finally see the source. A shade is drawn over a window that was left open. The breeze outside is pushing the shade away and then snapping it back. I open the door and enter the room. My pulse slows. I pull the shade and send it flying up. Sun blazes through the east-facing window, and a cool breeze bursts into the room. A painting of a lighthouse on the wall behind me shifts and nearly falls. I close the window before righting the painting. As I shift the canvas, something scrapes along the back of it. I think maybe the nail holding it up got yanked out a little by the breeze, so I lift the painting up for a look.

What I find stuns me. A safe. Behind a painting. It's so cliché that I'm shocked I hadn't thought to check for it before. After a quick peek into the living room, I put the painting on the floor and turn my attention to the safe. It's a combination lock. Probably three digits.

I decide to stick with cliché and try my father's birthday. No good. My mother's doesn't work either. Mine comes next and I'm slightly disappointed that it doesn't work. But I'm probably the one, aside from thieves, he wants to keep out of the safe, so that wouldn't make sense. I remember that my father is no good with remembering numbers. Despite being brilliant, he has trouble with phone numbers, street addresses and counting. So he's always writing things down. I look around the room. Where would he keep the number? It wouldn't be labeled, combination, but it also would be in a place where he couldn't confuse the number for something else.

The painting. The artist's signature was accompanied by a date. I kneel, looking at the bottom right corner. The signature is in a dull red, but the date—7-21-38—is a slightly brighter shade. They were put on at two different times! More than that, there is no way this painting was done in 1938. It's far too Bob Ross.

I spin the dial, entering the numbers and then turn the handle. The lock clunks and I let go. The safe swings open on its own.

Inside are several notebooks, folders, a small stack of money and a small felt pouch. I flip through the notebooks. They're field notes for his photo books. A few pages have love notes from my mom on them and I suspect this is the real reason he's kept them. There are three folders, each labeled for a member of the family. They contain birth certificates, social security cards and other legal documents. I notice I have no United States birth certificate, though there are other documents proving my citizenship. *There goes my chances of being president*, I think.

So far, it appears my parents really do have no secrets hidden in the house. I flip through the wad of hundred dollar bills, counting over one thousand dollars. All that's left is the felt pouch, which looks like it probably holds jewelry. I take it out and reach inside. The first object I find feels like a photo. I pull it out.

My parents are in the picture. Dad is standing behind mom, who looks exhausted. But she's smiling. Aimee is with her, by her side. And Dr. Clark is on the other side, next to my father. He's not really smiling at all. In fact, he doesn't look well. I turn the photo over and find a note.

To remember the extraordinary birth of your most unusual son. 9/2/1974 - Merrill

The word unusual churns a sick feeling in my stomach. But my curiosity over what heavy object still remains in the pouch distracts me. I turn the pouch over and let the contents slide onto the desk. It's a rock.

A simple stone. Granite, by the looks of it.

Then it occurs to me that this must be a piece of Antarctica.

Possibly collected the day I was born.

I pick it up and feel a surge of emotion. Thoughts and feelings race through my mind faster than I can comprehend. I feel strong one moment, lost the next. Afraid and angry. Resentful and full of wrath. But never happy. Never content. I am alone.

The experience is intense, and staggers me, but it lasts only a few seconds. As the feelings fade, a loud clap sounds out behind me.

I spin around with a shout and hurl the stone.

As soon as it leaves my hand, I return to my senses and realize what's about to happen. A window, which was also part way open like the one I had closed, shatters with a cacophony that only broken glass can make. The stone is stopped by the screen and lands atop a pile of glass. I cringe as the shards fall away, covering the window sill and floor.

Footsteps hit the floor above. The sound has roused my parents.

I quickly refill the safe, putting everything back in place. I put the photo back in the pouch and then reach for the stone. I pause before picking it up, wondering if I'm going to be overcome by emotion again. With all this broken glass and one of my parents on the way, that would be a very bad thing. But I see no choice, outside of getting caught, and pick up the stone.

Nothing happens.

I slide the stone in the pouch, cinch it shut and place it at the back of the safe before closing the safe door, spinning the lock and hanging the painting back in place. I hear my parent's door close. A second later the third step squeaks.

I dash into the living room and pick up the remote.

The fifth step squeaks and is followed by my father's voice. "Solomon? What was that noise?"

Back in the sunroom I place the remote inside the broken window and step back. My father's voice comes from the living room. "Solomon, what happened?"

He can see the glass and broken window.

He enters the sun room, glancing around. The painting holds his attention for just a brief moment, but then he's looking at the remote in the window. His annoyance is growing. "What—happened?"

"I threw the remote."

"I can see that."

"I thought there was a burglar."

The look in his eyes says several things to me. He thinks I'm nuts. He thinks I'm not ready to go to Antarctica. He thinks I'm lying. Of course, I am lying, but only partially.

"The shade slapped behind me. Look." I open the first window I'd closed and draw the shade. A moment later, the shade is pushed in by the wind and then sucked back out. The slap is loud and I see my father blink in surprise. "See?"

My father looks from the drawn shade to the broken window. He still doesn't look happy, but he's calming down. "Next time you think someone's in the house, you come get me."

I nod.

"And you can pay for the window out of your allowance."

I've already spent the money from my allowance on books, so

I'll be paying for the window with my birthday money. I think about the wad of hundred dollar bills in the safe, but decide it's in my best interest to keep that knowledge to myself.

"C'mon," he says. "Let's clean you up."

He turns and walks into the living room.

Clean me up? I look down and find blood on my hand. The cut isn't bad, but I didn't even feel it happen. My thoughts return to the stone and the way it made me feel—what it made me do. And for a moment, I'm not sure I want to go back to Antarctica after all. But then the craving to revisit my home returns and I know nothing will keep me away.

3

The weeks pass in a blur of anticipation. Life is a routine of eating, sleeping and studying, though I doubt I retain anything aside from the object of my fascination. I reread all my books on Antarctica, paying special attention to those written by Dr. Clark. I review a history of the continent and mark the beginnings and ends of all major expeditions in colored lines on my new, larger, map.

But I leave the map behind, which is fine with me because inside of twenty-four hours I will have set foot on the continent of my birth.

My leg shakes as I sit alone in the back seat of my father's pea soup colored sedan. I'm surrounded by luggage. If the car were to crash, I'm sure I wouldn't budge. But only ten minutes from home, the close confines are making me feel claustrophobic. I stuff as much of the luggage as I can behind my parents' seats.

The view out the window is unimpressive—mostly trees lining the highway—but I feel better.

When my father switches on the right turn signal, I forget all about my discomfort in the back seat. I stretch my neck up, looking out the front windshield. Exit five. Portsmouth, New Hampshire. I wonder if one of them has to pee, but I see no restaurants or gas stations. And we've only been on the road for thirty minutes. This should have been a straight shot to Logan airport in Boston.

"Where are we going?" I ask.

My dad turns back. He's smiling. "Just a quick detour."

I look at my watch. There's still plenty of time. But my curiosity is piqued. "To where?"

"You'll see," says mom, but she's got a jovial tone in her voice. Once again, they know something I don't and find it humorous. My stomach churns for a moment, but I distract myself with thoughts of home. I want to enjoy every moment of this trip. Instead of watching the road, I poke at the fabric hanging down from the car's ceiling. Just as I'm starting to wonder what kind of weak glue the manufacturer used, the car stops.

I look up. A large wrought iron gate is opening up before us. That's when I notice we're at the top of a very tall hill. The car pulls forward. The driveway is long and lined by grass that's still green, despite the frigid late fall weather. The house is a brick colonial, clearly old—perhaps early 1700s—but impeccably maintained.

"Who lives here?" I whisper under my breath. The question

was rhetorical and directed at myself, but my father hears. He puts the car in park and turns around with an arm up on the back of his seat. The smile on his face tells me that this detour is for me. His next words confirm it.

"Merrill Clark lives here. His family is joining us."

Mom and Dad exit the car as a man steps out of the front door. I can't see his face because Mom is already hugging him. Dad shakes his hand next. I'm in the front seat now, shaking with excitement and fear. For other New England kids, this would be like meeting Larry Bird or Wade Boggs. I'm going to be spending the next few weeks with my hero. And I'm desperate to make a good impression.

Should I quote him? Should I tell him my theories on ancient Antarctican civilizations? Should I ask him to sign my copy of *Antarktos*?

I decide, push the car door open and step out. Before I know what's happened, I fall forward, reach out and land on the paved driveway, which feels harder in the bitter chill. I land with a slap.

The pain is sharp, rising from my hands, traveling up my arms and descending to my gut. The blow has sucked away my breath. But I hold back my tears. I don't gasp for air. I don't even look at my parents. If they're laughing, I'll cry for sure. So I focus on figuring out what happened. A quick look back answers that question. My shoelace is wedged in the car door. I yank at it, but instead of coming free, it snaps in half. I fall back, hitting my head.

I feel a growl rising in my throat. I've never been more embarrassed. I want to go home.

"You okay?"

The voice doesn't belong to either of my parents and certainly not to Dr. Clark. I turn my head toward the person standing above me. A girl. Her skin is a deep tan, but her hair, tied back in a tight bun, is as blond as mine. She smiles down at me and for a moment, I hold my breath. She's stunning. She's a girl. And she's smiling at me. This is a first.

She reaches down and takes my hand. I'm too flabbergasted to realize she's pulling me to my feet, so she ends up doing most of the work. She's strong. Stronger than me, that's for sure.

Once I'm standing again, some sense returns. I quickly look to my parents and Dr. Clark. They're still talking, oblivious to what just happened.

"Don't worry," the girl says, "no one saw you."

I turn back to the girl, seeing her for who she is. The dark skin. The blond hair. And her eyes. "Mirabelle Clark," I say.

"Solomon Vincent," she says. "But I'm pretty sure we're supposed to say our own names, not each other's."

When she starts shaking my hand, I realize she hadn't let go. My hand begins to sweat so I break away from the handshake, feigning an itch on my head. I can tell by her smile that she sees through my ruse. To her credit, and my relief, she doesn't mention it. Instead, she heads toward our parents and motions me to follow.

"C'mon," she says. "Introduce me to your dad."

My dad? I think. *What's so great about*—? Then, I see the camera around her neck. My father is a photographer for *National Geographic*. Many of his photos from their Clark Station years are in *Antarktos*. If Mirabelle wants to be a photographer, then my dad is probably her hero as much as her father is mine.

Knowing this is a great relief. For a moment I worried that I would be constantly paired with Mirabelle throughout the trip, unable to pursue my interests because our parents were trying to play Antarctican matchmakers. But as I watch her walk away, I feel my face flush. Not only is she pretty, but she spoke to me with a kindness I hadn't yet experienced from a girl my age.

In fact, she's got me so distracted that when I'm introduced to Dr. Clark, I totally botch the quote, making myself look like a buffoon. As they pack the cars, I'm told there are chocolate chip cookies on the kitchen counter if I want one. I don't, but I want to be out of sight so much that if they had said there were chocolate covered locusts in the kitchen, I would have accepted the offer just the same. I suppose I'm like an ostrich, hiding my head in the sand. I sometimes wonder if this habit will make me a pushover as an adult, too, but I've seen my parents ignore enough problems around the house to know that even grownups sometimes have trouble facing life's challenges. And I'm only thirteen. So I'll put my head inside a cookie jar or metaphorical sand and not feel bad about it.

Like the outside of the house, the inside is old, but well maintained. The hardwood, which is everywhere—floors, mantles, railing, stairs—shines with a polish that looks new, but I suspect is just cared for. Even with the polish, I don't feel like I can't touch anything. Justin's mom has a room in their house that we can't even walk through. A living room in which no one lives. This is a great inconvenience, because the living room leads to the den, where the TV is, and instead of walking straight through, we have to walk around the entire first floor.

This house doesn't feel untouchable. This home is lived in. This home is loved.

Straight through the hallway at the center of the house, on the kitchen counter, I see the cookies. I still don't want one, but if someone follows me in, I don't want to look like a klutz, a doofus *and* a liar.

On my way to the kitchen, almost every floor-board I step on creaks. *Ninjas would hate this house*, I think before picking up one of the coaster-sized cookies. I take a reluctant bite. The brown sugar melts in my mouth, followed by a still warm burst of semi-sweet goodness. I change my mind about the cookie and pick up a second.

"Don't eat too many," a woman says, spinning me around on my heels.

Her skin is two shades darker than Mirabelle's but her smile seems even brighter. I recognize her immediately. My father took a stunning photo of her once, sitting on a glacier wrapped in a blanket, having a picnic. Only, that's not why I recognize her. "Hello, Mrs. Clark. How are you?"

She stops, puts a hand to her ample hip and says, "Well, aren't you the polite one."

I'm not sure what to say, but I'm not nearly as nervous around Mrs. Clark as I am around Merrill, or their daughter. I continue with a compliment. "These are really good."

"You know, as much as I know everyone loves these cookies,

you're the first person to compliment them."

This strikes me as odd, given how good they are. She takes out a plastic bag, loads it with three more cookies, takes the second out of my hand, adds it to the bag and hands it to me. She gives me a wink that lets me know we're in cahoots. I nod and stuff the cookies into my cargo pants pocket.

"Thank you, Mrs. Clark."

"Enough with the Mrs. stuff. Call me Aimee."

I've never once in my life been invited to call an adult by their first name. I heard once that an art teacher at my former high school allowed the students to call her by her first name. But someone told her she couldn't and she quit. I remember thinking she was silly for quitting, but having now experienced the sense of pride over using an adult's first name, I understand. It's a gift. An acknowledgement of not being superior simply for being older.

"I like how you spell your name." Then I try it on for size. "Aimee." But I drag the E sound out.

She laughs. "I have my mother to thank for the spelling. I like it now, but kids made fun of me a lot for it when I was your age."

I think about the kids in my school, imagine what they'd come up with, and nod. They'd probably still make fun of her name. They certainly made fun of mine. Solomon. That alone could be bad enough. But my middle name—Ull—what were my parents thinking?

Granted, I appreciate the significance; Ull was the son of the Norse god, Thor. He was the god of winter, which is how I ended up with the name. Being born in a place of perpetual winter, I suppose it makes sense. Ull was also the god of death, the chase, combat, archery, hunting and trapping. I'll never be good at any of those things, but at least my light complexion and ultra-blond hair fit the Viking look. Still, being named for a Norse god does not do wonders for a person who's already socially black-listed.

She sits on a bar stool and starts on a cookie. I perch myself in the stool across from her like we're old chums.

"So how nervous are you?" she asks.

"Nervous?"

"About going home."

I feel like she has somehow torn me open and looked at my soul. To everyone else I've appeared nothing but excited. In truth, I'm fearful of what I'll find in Antarctica. I can't fully ex-plain it, but I think it has to do with my high expectations. It's like when you go to a movie everyone has said is amazing, but it's only so-so, and you end up hating it because of your raised expec-tations. I'm afraid that will happen in Antarctica, because I expect my homecoming to be magical. Even I know that's stupid. Any real magic done in the past was simply science ahead of its time used on naïve people. Antarctica will not be magical, but I wish to my core that it will be. Of course, my rock throwing incident also has me worried that I'll become a raging psychopath the moment I set foot on the continent.

"A lot," I admit. "Part of me wants to spend a lifetime there, learning about the place, searching for its history."

"For your history."

I feel a wash of embarrassment. "I know anything found on

Antarctica isn't really my history, but—"

"You were born there," she says firmly. "You probably have a legal claim to the continent, too. The history of that place is as much yours as South Africa is mine."

"You were born in South Africa?"

She nods. "I spent the first year of my life there. And I still feel a strong connection to the country even though I have no memory of the place and have yet to return."

"You can't remember it?"

"I was only one when my parents came to the States."

I look at the plate of cookies, feeling awkward. Once again, she looks inside me and sees what no one else ever has. She gasps. "You can remember Antarctica, can't you?"

I give the slightest tilt of my head. I can. "Clark Station smelled like rust. There was a lot of it on the walls, and around the doors. My parents' room was decorated with Indian wall hangings—India Indian, not American Indian."

Her open mouth confirms the accuracy of what I've said. I remember much more, but I've made my point.

"I knew you were smart, Solomon, but I had no idea..." She puts her cookie down. "Do your parents know?"

I shake my head, no. They already treat me special enough.

She nods as though she understands why, and I think she really might.

"What was the very first thing you remember?" she asks.

"You mean after I was born?"

Her eyes go wide for a moment. A wide smile follows as she realizes I've just made a joke. She picks up the cookie again and takes a bite. "Yes, after you were born."

"First memory?"

"Very first."

I pause. I know the answer. But I don't want to freak her out. I think she'll see through it if I try to lie. So I tell the truth. "You."

The cookie falls from her hand.

"Your face," I say. "You delivered me. You were smiling just like you are now. When I saw you, when I looked into your eyes, I felt...loved."

"And you stopped crying," she says, and I can see tears in her eyes. Good to know I'm not the only crybaby going on this trip.

"I remember our eyes meeting," she continues. "And then you just stopped crying. I thought it was a fluke, but you stared up at me so intently."

"And then Dad took me," I say, "and I didn't like it."

"He wasn't used to holding a baby, never mind a newborn."

"Let's go, you two!" Dr. Clark yells from the front door.

Aimee wipes her eyes and dumps the cookies into a Tupperware container. She picks up a bag and heads for the door. "Let's get a move on, Sol. I'll keep quiet about your memories if you keep quiet about those cookies in your pocket. Otherwise we'll have a riot on our hands."

I smile as I follow her to the door. For the first time in a very long time, I've made a friend. And it's not Merrill, whom I admire so much, or Mirabelle, who is age appropriate and beautiful, it's Aimee Clark, who is not only the first person I met upon entering the world, but is also the nicest.

I make a mental note to be far away from her when I step off the plane and onto Antarctica. If I get violent, I don't want her anywhere near me.

4

The car ride to Logan Airport is cramped. Not only am I still surrounded by luggage, but I'm also wedged in tight with Mirabelle Clark. I have never been this close to a girl for this length of time. I'll be dehydrated from sweating before we even reach the dry air of the airplane cabin.

But it could be worse. She doesn't smell like a girl. Few things irritate me more than the chemical scents women and girls douse themselves in. Scented soaps, perfumes, deodorants—they're all bad. The worst ones are those made from animal pheromones. Don't people realize what they're spraying on themselves? Gross.

She also seems to have no interest in talking to me. Instead she's playing twenty questions with my dad. More like one hundred and twenty questions. They've been talking photography since they shook hands. Dad seems to be enjoying the conversation as much as Mirabelle. The only interest I showed in photography was when I read all of dad's camera manuals and how-to guides. As a result, there are several points in the conversation when I could correct both of them on the proper way to light, frame or filter a shot. But I learned to keep my mouth shut about such things long ago. No one likes a know-it-all.

What stinks about the current scenario is that I have yet to talk to Dr. Clark. My dad said we'd get to talk on the plane, but I'm starting to doubt it. He doesn't seem all that interested in me. Back at the house, our eyes met and he looked quickly away, like he wanted nothing to do with me. I'm sure I read his face right. I've seen that look before. Several times.

But Dr. Clark is not the reason for this trip. I try to remind myself that. Unlike Larry Bird, Dr. Clark isn't used to having young fans or being a role model. He may positively loathe children, though I doubt it. Mirabelle seems too well adjusted.

In fact, I think I'll be okay with her joining us on this trip. I can't stand most kids my age, but she's well spoken, fairly intelligent, kind and pretty. Though that last quality is a drawback and will probably prevent us from every really being friends.

I'm suddenly being ribbed by Mirabelle's sharp elbow. At first it hurts, but then I remember whose elbow it is and it tickles so much I flinch away. But she and dad are laughing and don't notice. Was there a joke at my expense? I'll never know because they're back to talking about cameras—Polaroid this time.

Before I can tune out the conversation again I'm punched in the shoulder. It hurts as much as one of Justin's slugs and I have to fight the urge to cry out. But Mirabelle is smiling in my face.

"What do you think about Polaroid?" she asks.

And there it is. I'm in the conversation. I'm not sure how to answer. I don't know what's been said so far or if I'll contradict it. Mirabelle has no patience for my pause.

"Well?"

"The first Polaroid camera was sold in 1947. It uses self-developing film that works when microscopic crystals of iodoquinine sulfate—"

"No, no, no," she says, "that's what you *know*. What's your opinion of the cameras? Of the photos they take? What do you *think*?"

"Oh, well. I like to shake them," I say. It's true. Vigorously shaking a Polaroid photo gives me some kind of strange satisfaction. I have yet to determine why.

She's nodding, but has a look on her face that says, *who doesn't?* And she's waiting for more.

"They provide instant gratification, which is fun I suppose, but the images are small, not nearly as clear and seem to fade quickly."

She punches me again. "There, you see?" She's talking to my dad. "Exactly what I said, but more intelligent sounding. Not great quality, but instant gratification."

Before I realize it, she's got her head on my shoulder. Her curling blond hair tickles my cheek. And a Polaroid camera rises in front of us. As my nervousness at her close proximity rises to near panic status, a flash of light blinds me. While my eyes recover, I feel a faint breeze and hear a repetitious flapping. When I finally recover, I see Mirabelle leaning over, writing on something with a permanent marker. Then she's back up and handing me a Polaroid picture.

"The first of many memories," she says.

I take the picture and look at it, dumbfounded by what I see. There's Mirabelle, smiling wide, eyes unbelievably dark, head on my shoulder. And then there's me. Despite my nervous jitters I look happy. Really happy. In fact, this might be the first photo of me sporting a genuine smile.

Beneath the photo, Mirabelle has written: Mira and Sol, 1987.

"Mira," I say, reading her name.

"That's my name, don't wear it out," she says.

"Why not Mirabelle?"

"Kind of a mouthful. Does your family call you Solomon?"

They don't. I shake my head, no.

"Well, we're both lucky. Our names sound just as good shortened as they do long."

My eyebrows rise involuntarily. "You like my name?"

"Are you serious? King Solomon the wise and his legendary mines. Solomon Grundy—the nursery rhyme and evil comic-book zombie super villain."

Then she's singing, "Any hemisphere. No man's land. Ain't no asylum here. King Solomon he never lived round here."

"What's that?" I ask.

"The Clash," she says.

"Clash of the Titans?" Harryhausen was a genius with stop motion, but I don't recognize the lines as being from any of his films.

She gives me a funny look. "You don't listen to music much,

do you?"

"Only what Justin brings over. He's my friend."

She digs in her backpack. "I kinda figured that." She pulls out a bright yellow cassette walkman. She extends the earphones as far as they'll go and stretches them over both our heads, one side on her right ear, the other on my left. Then she hits play and I hear a tune similar to the one she was just singing.

I don't hear the words at first because I'm distracted by the softness of Mira's cheek up against mine. She's bobbing her head to the music and our skin is rubbing. As I grow accustomed to the closeness, I hear the beat again. Then the tune. To my surprise, I like it. Then I hear the lyrics, and I'm not so sure.

There ain't no need for ya. Go straight to Hell boys.
Go straight to Hell boys.

5

Logan is a whirlwind of confusion. I'm not sure how my parents can navigate through the terminals. But they do. And after checking our luggage and Dr. Clark's massive amount of supplies—so much that he needed to get special permission to bring them—we're on the plane and in the air.

I sit in a window seat, watching the East Coast pass below us as we head south. My mom and dad are sitting next to me and coax me into eating a small bag of peanuts and drinking a Sprite. I'd be worried if this was all I had to eat—the airline food is hideous—but I know Mom's carry-on is full of food and drink. As my father's photography assistant it's her job to be prepared for anything, which includes my father's voracious appetite.

About an hour into the flight, people become restless and a sort of musical chairs breaks out. Some people move to unoccupied rows, seeking solitude. Other people shift spots so they're sitting next to friends or relatives they weren't seated with. About five minutes into the shift, my parents are on their feet.

"I'm going to visit with Aimee," mom says. "Your father needs to pee. Won't be long."

I shrug, not really caring where they're going and turn my attention back to the view. I can no longer see the ocean. That's right, our stop-over is in Texas. Then Peru. Then... As my thoughts turn to Antarctica, I feel my Dad return to his seat next to me. But something's not right.

I sniff. The person next to me doesn't smell like my Dad. I turn, expecting to see Mira, but it's not her either. It's Dr. Clark. He looks over at me, his dark hair ruffled in the back from leaning on his seat. And there is something odd about his eyes. Not the color, they're a perfectly normal blue. It's the tightness around the edges. He looks nervous.

I know I must, too, because he forces a smile. I return it with one I'm sure looks equally as awkward. He clears his throat. "Sorry," he says. "I'm just excited to meet you."

"Excited to meet me?" I'm honestly thrown by this.

"You are the modern equivalent of what I've spent most of my career searching for."

"An Antarctican."

He nods.

"That doesn't make me special. If anything it makes me stranger than I already am."

"Strange, my boy, is a good thing," he says. And I can tell he's

not joking. "We live in a world of mediocrity, of settling for so-
ciety's norms. Anything outside of that is deemed strange. If
you're smart. If you're creative. If you simply just want something
different for your life. Of course, you're all three of those, aren't
you?"

"So, I'm stranger than most?"

"*Better* than most," he says with a wink.

I can tell he's relaxing, which is good, because it's helping me
relax, too.

"We weren't put on this Earth to be stagnant."

I think about his word choice. Stagnant in the current context
means a lack of progress. But when talking about the physical
world it means things are going foul from standing still. It's a
loaded sentence. "So our brains will rot if we aren't strange?"

"Precisely." He laughs. I smile. This is going much better then
when I fell on my face.

"But I'm not really different because I was born on Antarctica,
am I?"

His smile fades some and I know the answer to my question.
He thinks I am different. More so than makes any sense. "Why?"
I ask, but then think, *because he knows—he was there when I was
born.*

"There is so much about Antarctica we don't know," he says.
"The vast majority of the continent, which is the size of the United States, is buried beneath the ice. What little is exposed has
been all but scoured clean by the katabatic winds."

Katabatic winds are created when gravity pulls dense air down
a slope from higher elevations. Since Antarctica is essentially a big

mound of snow, this is commonplace. The winds can reach speeds faster than any hurricane and a few of the people who have been lost on the continent disappeared into a cloud of rushing snow carried by the winds. Just one of the many dangers the continent offers visitors.

Hello and welcome to Antarctica, I think, *try not to get killed!*

"But we know people visited Antarctica, even lived on Antarctica, more than six thousand years ago."

"The Piri Reis map," I say.

He nods, growing excited. "Not only does the map show animals reminiscent of cattle and mink, it also shows other strange creatures and odd looking primates. Even a wall of some kind."

"I've often wondered if those were just embellishments by the artist," I admit.

"That is a possibility," he says, "but I highly doubt it. The map's details are better than any modern map, and it depicts the coast of an Antarctica free of ice. Given its geographic accuracy and the fact that the continent would have had to be ice free at the time, there is no reason to doubt that the land was populated. The map itself proves that ancient humans visited the continent."

"Makes sense," I say. "But that doesn't make me any different."

"You might change your mind when we get there," he says. "There's something magical about the place. And I think a little bit of that magic was instilled in you when you were born."

Magic? I can't believe a man like Merrill Clark would buy into such things. I can't stop myself from asking. "You don't believe in magic do you?"

"Not in the sense you're thinking," Dr. Clark says. "Not the hocus pocus, bunny-in-the-hat kind. I do believe in the supernatural. In God. But that's not what I'm talking about either. It's hard to describe. What I do know is that something truly strange happened when you were born. Something that still excites me when I think about it. Perhaps we'll understand the science behind it someday, but—"

"You think it will happen again when I go back, don't you?" I ask.

"Can't say I haven't considered the possibility. But you were on the continent for several weeks before it was safe to move you. The event never repeated itself, though the storm that eventually buried the station didn't let up for years."

His eyes drift to the seat in front of him. I can tell he's remembering something. He snaps out of his thoughts and says, "The truth is, I hope nothing happens when you set foot on Antarctica."

Like becoming overwhelmed by negative emotions and going on a killing spree, I think, but then I force the concern from my mind. This is the moment I have been waiting for. Clark knows everything my parents have hid from me. His memory is the safe I need to crack. "What happened?" I ask.

"You've heard, I'm sure. About the howling."

I nod, but the look in my eyes betrays how little I actually know. I heard about the howling on two occasions, both at gatherings my parents hosted, from people whose memories of the past were diluted by alcohol at the time.

He chuckles. "Have they really not told you yet?"

My anger at my parents' silence increases and my voice oozes frustration. "Dad says the only howling was my mother."

He looks down the aisle in both directions and then leans in close. He's clearly about to tell me something my parents wouldn't want me to know. When he speaks, his eyes are wide and his voice is animated. "Well, I'm sure that's all *he* could hear, but the rest of us...it was like a Viking war horn sounding from all around. I felt terrified when I heard it. Then the wind came. Tore the roof away from one of the research buildings. The wind carried snow so thick I couldn't see more than a foot. It's a miracle I made it back at all."

"You were out in the storm?"

He's quiet for a moment, lost in thought again. "I was," he whispers. "I was. And I'm the only one who saw it."

Saw what? I think, but he doesn't give me time to ask.

"You know about the ice sheet breaking free?"

I dip my head down in a nod.

"I was there. When it broke. A flash of blue, like lightning contained in the ice, shot down the hill toward the ocean. When it reached the edge of the continent, where the ice floated on top of the ocean, the energy burst, dissipating suddenly. The crack of the ice was so loud it hurt my ears. The split spread to the horizon in both directions and then it was free, a six hundred square mile iceberg formed at the moment of your birth. The wind came just after that, then the snow. I was bedridden for days afterwards. Nearly lost a toe. I have a ringing in my ears. I've never seen another storm like it since." He fixes his eyes on mine. "How do you think you got your name?"

"Solomon?"

"Ull, the god of winter. You descended on Antarctica that day and brought your storm with you." He gives me a smile. "Don't let your father fool you. He knows everything I've told you is true."

"You think that's why they named me, Ull?"

"I have no doubt."

"Why?"

He laughs at this. "Because I gave you the name."

This has me stunned. Dr. Merrill Clark named me? Ull, the god of winter. It sounds unbelievable, but now that I'm thinking about it, it makes too much sense. My father has very little interest in ancient cultures, religions or history in general. He's more concerned with capturing the here and now on film. But Dr. Clark, he's an anthropologist who has written extensively on the ancient religions of the world, including the Norse gods. He's telling the truth.

The insanity of all this has me shaken. For a moment, I understand why Mom and Dad kept all this from me. It's so...unbelievable. So strange, even for me. If not for my experience with the Antarctic stone in my father's safe, I might have discounted everything Clark said. But if it's true...

I shake my head. Though I have a thousand more questions, I feel overwhelmed and need to process what I've heard. So I whittle my queries down to one and ask, "My parents kept this from me my whole life. Why are you telling me now?"

"To prepare you."

"For what?"

"In case it happens again."

6

I spend the next two flights getting to know Merrill, Aimee and Mira in a kind of round robin rotation where everyone switches seats and either strikes up a new conversation or continues an unfinished one. I'm sitting with Mira now, and it's dark, so she's sleeping, but I'm wide awake. In fact, I don't think I've ever been more awake in my life.

Not only am I on a small plane over a very, very cold ocean between Peru and Antarctica, not only am I sitting next to a girl whose presence still has me feeling funny, not only am I going home to Antarctica, but I'm now also afraid that the whole continent will explode beneath my feet the moment I step down from the plane.

I've had sixteen conversations since my first with Dr. Clark and not one could distract me from his account of my birth. So much so that I can't remember long portions of those conversations. Me, the kid with the perfect memory, can't remember! I must have tuned them out entirely.

For a moment I worry if I made a bad impression somewhere along the way. Maybe I stared dumbfounded while someone spoke? Maybe I drooled like I was in some kind of vegetative state?

According to the kids at school, that's what I look like all the time, so I decide not to worry about it.

A yawn grips my body. When it lets go, I'm exhausted. I look around the cabin. Mira isn't the only one asleep. Aimee and my parents are too. The only one who's not is Merrill. He's staring out his window.

I wonder what he's looking at. It's dark outside, so there shouldn't be much of a view, and he's looking down, not up, so he can't be looking at the moon. He's suddenly aware of me. He motions toward my window. He wants me to look. But Mira has the shade drawn.

I look back to Merrill. He's insistent so I know there's something worth seeing, and I know he won't mind that I have to lean over his daughter to look. I reach over and raise the shade. Darkness fills the window. Just like I thought.

I lean forward, trying not wake Mira, but her nappy hair has exploded into a blond pompom around her head that is impossible to avoid. I pause, expecting her to wake up, but she remains asleep. I press my face against the window and look toward the front of the plane. At first I see nothing, but then, with my eyes adjusted to the dark, a wall of white emerges. Antarctica is just ahead, glowing in the moonlight like a continent-sized ghost. Beyond the sheet of white, an arc of dark blue fills the sky. The day is coming.

I'm dazzled by the sight for a moment. Until my fears return. Then I feel like I'm going to puke. I feel the same way when I go to the dentist. I sit in the chair, eyeing the room for any signs of drills or needles. If I see them, well, the physical reaction is severe.

Thankfully, I'm distracted by Mira, who has just stretched herself awake and in doing so has wrapped her arms around me. She pulls me down, bringing my face just inches from hers. My heart is pounding. Is she going to kiss me? I've never kissed a girl! Dr. Clark is probably watching! But...her eyes are closed. Then they're open, looking into mine, growing wide.

"Hello," she says, sounding confused and embarrassed. Then she notices her arms around me. She lets go and looks positively panic stricken.

"Hi," I say.

"What...happened?"

"I was looking out the window," I say. I've managed to pull my face away from hers, but am still too frozen to move away. "I think you grabbed me when you stretched."

"Mmm," she says, looking at the window.

I can tell she doesn't want to talk about it anymore so I change the subject. "We're almost there. Look for yourself."

She moves to the window and I force myself to sit back in my seat. As I'm sitting, I glance back at Dr. Clark expecting to see a father's glare. Instead he's still staring out his own window. This eases my anxiety some, but the adrenaline flowing through my body as a result of almost being kissed will take some time to dissipate. I look at Mira, noticing her very full lips. Perhaps a long time to dissipate.

The "Fasten Your Seatbelts" sign glows red and the captain's voice booms from the intercom. "Ladies and gentlemen, we are making our final approach to Williams Field, Antarctica. Please return your seats to their upright position and fasten your seatbelts. If you were smart enough to unpack your winter gear, put it on now. You're going to want it when we open the doors."

Everyone is awake now. Putting up their seats. Buckling their seatbelts. Rubbing their eyes. But no one is putting on any snow gear. I wonder if the captain knew this and was trying to be funny.

I feel the plane bank and then descend. I look past Mira. Through the window I see flat, white ice. The stars are just barely visible in the now navy blue sky. Morning on Antarctica.

The landing is smooth despite the runway being nothing more than densely packed snow. I wonder if the whole runway will break free and float away when I step on it. Even if it did, that wouldn't matter much. The whole runway sits atop a sheet of ice that moves inexorably over and into eighteen hundred feet of ocean. Just a few years ago, in 1985, they had to relocate the entire airfield to its current location. As long as the frozen conveyor belt continues to slide away from the continent, they'll have to move the airfield every fifteen years or so.

The plane comes to a stop and the captain enters the cabin.

He's dressed in snow pants and a white parka. "Listen up folks. It's cold out there. Colder than many of you will have felt in your entire lives. There's a transport waiting for you outside. They'll take you to Willy Town while we unload your equipment. Gear up at Willy Town and visit the galley for your first taste of Antarctican cuisine. Any questions?"

No one has any.

The captain turns to the outer hatch and looks back at us. "Just do me a favor and don't stand around in the cold. No one likes cutting off fingers, but we have to do it occasionally."

The door clanks open. A burst of air and snow slams into the cabin but then quickly abates. A lot of people make loud "brrr" sounds and start rubbing their arms. I head for the door.

The captain gives me a once over. I'm dressed in black pants and a black turtleneck. As I realize my hair is floating around my head thanks to a buildup of head-rest static, I expect the captain to make an Andy Warhol joke, but this man is sinister. He aims below the belt.

"This isn't a beatnik poetry session," he says. "Get in the heated cab and bring a coat next time."

What he doesn't know is that I have a coat. I'm sure my mother is fishing it out right now. But I can't wait. And I want to do this on my own. If something happens, I don't want anyone to see it. I don't want anyone to be in striking distance, either.

I nod to the captain and head outside. A burst of Antarctican air hits me before I'm halfway down the steps. I breathe it in. I let it out. My muscles relax. A smile creeps onto my face.

I stop at the last step, looking at the packed ice just ten inches away. I move to step on it slowly, as I would ice that was a half inch thick, but am bumped from behind by one of the other passengers I did not meet.

"Are you nuts?" the woman says as she rushes past me, headed for the Sno-Cat transport waiting ten feet away.

I lose my balance and fall forward, landing hard on my feet.

Nothing happens.

I wait.

Still nothing.

More people are rushing past now.

Relief floods my system, further relaxing me. Maybe Clark was wrong about me? Maybe my parents had nothing to hide?

Then I look up at the plane and see Dr. Clark. He's looking out the window at me, a big grin on his face. *Nothing happened*, I think, *so what's he so excited about?*

Another passenger rushes by, this one dressed in a thick coat, but just as chilled as the others.

That's when I realize what Dr. Clark has already figured out.

I'm not cold. Not at all.

7

The next day is so rushed and chaotic I rarely have a chance to remember I'm on Antarctica. It's more like a snow camp for adults. I spend the first half of the day in a distracted stupor, trying to figure out how I seem to be immune to temperature changes. I know I felt cold at home. I remember feeling hot on the plane. But here, where I should be shivering with everyone else, I feel nothing beyond a comfortable warmth I peg around seventy degrees. With no explanations forthcoming, and no chance to discuss the development with Dr. Clark, I set my mind to my surroundings, and I absorb what I can of Antarctica.

There are more people than I expected. A few hundred populate Willy Town. At the center of the town are a few large, but moveable, buildings. Surrounding the buildings are rows of large metal shipping containers that store supplies, serve as homes and utterly devastate the landscape. The rows of bright red, green, orange and yellow look like the *Breakout* video game I used to play on my Atari.

After everyone is dressed, we shuffle from building to building, suffering through hours of briefings on weather, safety and schedules. Even Dr. Clark, who has spent more hours on the continent than most, must endure the endless lectures. The one interesting bit of news I learn is that my family is an official part of the Clark expedition, at least temporarily. We're not here as tourists. None of these people are. We're here to work, or at least that's what everyone has been told. By the time we're done, most people have warmed up, but now everyone is hungry and night is beginning to fall.

When given the option to eat food from our supplies or visit Willy Field Tavern, both my parents vote emphatically for the tavern. This comes as a surprise to me. In my lifetime I've never seen either of them take a drink. And they certainly haven't gone to any bars. But they seem eager to visit the tavern and become slightly jovial as we maneuver through the Jujubes-colored maze.

We arrive at the tavern five minutes later. The white building sports angled walls and looks like it could fall over with the slightest shift of the ice. Two metal supports on the side validate this concern. But my parents and the Clarks all enter without pause, so I follow.

The inside is like something out of a movie— Bob's Country Bunker from *The Blues Brothers*. A real cowboy establishment. Even has horns mounted on the wall. Fluorescent beer signs adorn the walls and a thick cloud of cigarette smoke hangs in the air. I try not to cough, but can't stop it. Mira is coughing now too. She gives me a look of disgust, apparently as unimpressed as I am.

As our parents lead us to the back of the establishment, I scan the room. Most of the patrons are men—large hairy men wearing thick, brightly colored, full-body snow suits. The few women in the room are surrounded by men, many of whom are staring at my mother.

I suddenly feel hot. I had yet to feel any kind of temperature change since our arrival, but now my cheeks are burning up. It's not the air, though, it's my emotions. An uncommon rage has struck me. I glare at one of the men eyeing my mom and catch his attention. I'm not sure what my face looks like, but the man actually turns away.

That's when I notice more than a few people are looking at me. You'd think Mira, with her dark skin and light hair would attract more attention. Even the bartender is glaring now. He's just standing there, rubbing a glass clean like it's covered in sap, staring at me. One man, sporting a long white beard, sits in what appears to be a barber shop chair. When he sees me, he starts spinning the chair. With every rotation he meets my eyes again.

My anger fades rapidly, replaced by fear. These people strike me as wild. Some seem positively unhinged. Then I remember that there are no real laws on Antarctica. This isn't the United States. There is no sovereignty here. Well, some would say I have sovereignty here, but I don't think that would go over well with this lot.

We sit in a booth at the back of the room where a vent in the ceiling holds the smoke cloud at bay. It's a tight fit, but the six of us manage, with the Clarks on one side, my family on the other.

"Kinda creepy in here," Mira says to me.

I look out at the room and several people look away. "Very," I say.

"What'll it be," Dr. Clark says, "Penguin Club or Salisbury Seal?"

I glance down at the menu. Sure enough, normal meats have been replaced with the Antarctican equivalent. Penguin is no doubt chicken. Seal is beef. The fish, well, that's probably fish. "Penguin," I say without missing a beat.

"Attaboy," Dr. Clark says with something sounding so close to pride that I second guess my assessment of the menu.

The waiter, who also happens to be the bartender, appears at my side. He looks down at me while he speaks to the group. "What can I git for ya?" His voice is deep and rough. His accent southern, maybe Louisianan.

Dr. Clark and my father place the orders. The man seems to be keeping one eye on the pad of paper he's writing on and the other on me. He stabs his pen onto the pad as he finishes, takes one step away and then stops. He turns back to the table.

"You look familiar," he says.

"We were here thirteen years ago," my father says. "Several years in a row. Ate here more than a few times."

"Wasn't talkin' a you," the man says, then looks at Merrill, who is about to speak. "Or you."

He's talking about me. As I grow nervous my mind plays through several rapid-fire scenarios, most of them ending with this man and several customers beating me to a pulp. My body tenses. Beneath the table, I feel my fingers tightening like they did that day in the living room. Like I have claws.

What's wrong with me?

"You been here before?" the man asks.

"No," I answer quickly, wishing the man would leave so we can eat and leave the smoke filled tavern.

He grunts, still looking at me.

My father, who seems nonplussed by the situation, nudges me He hasn't said a word, but I quickly understand what he's telling me. I *have* been here before. But I don't feel like talking about that for some reason.

Mira, on the other hand, does. "He was born here."

The man's eyes widen, and when they do I can see that one of his eyes is glass. He hadn't been looking at me while he wrote. This calms me some, despite the grossness of his lazy, fake eye. He stares down at me for a moment. "Over at Clark Station?"

"Yes," Dr. Clark says with a big smile, clearly happy that the man remembers me after all this time. "I'm Dr. Clark."

But the man pays him no attention. "You going to be here long?"

The question is directed at me. I'm not sure if he's talking about the tavern, Willy Town or the continent. With a shaky voice, I answer, "We're staying the night in town and heading out in the morning." I don't say where we're going because I'm not sure.

The man grunts, heads back toward the bar and says over his shoulder, "Welcome home, Ull."

Everyone at the table is stunned to silence. Then Mom is smiling and laughing. "I had no idea they'd remember you!"

"First and only child born on the continent," Dad says. "Probably hard to forget."

All four adults are talking now, but I don't hear what they're saying. I'm still rooted to my seat, gripping the edges with my fingers. The rest of the tavern has fallen silent, all eyes on me.

Mira has noticed as well. She surveys the room and turns back to me. She looks nervous. In her fear, I find strength. I meet the eyes of those looking at me and nod my head in acknowledgement. This seems to break the spell and everyone returns to their business—eating, drinking, carousing.

Mira has seen the change in my body language and shoots me a look. I'm not sure where the will to face down a tavern full of the world's thickest, hairiest men, came from. I can't stare down a golden retriever. But I did. I give her a smile and she returns it.

I pull out an imaginary notepad and start writing on it with an imaginary pen, "Note to self, girls like it when boys stare down freaky old drunk people."

Mira laughs out loud. A moment later, I feel her foot touching mine. This would normally cause me to flinch away or excuse myself to the bathroom, but I don't move it. I allow the connection to be made. It's subtle and our skin is separated by multiple layers of socks and boots. But we both feel the pressure and for a thirteen year old boy and a twelve year old girl, this is a significant step. I think. I've actually never done this before.

I smile back at her. In a matter of minutes I've managed to speak to the freakiest man I've ever met, stare down a room of drunks who all seem to know who I am and initiate physical contact with a girl that I now suspect will kiss me before I leave this continent. *I'm changing*, I think. And while I'm not sure where my newfound confidence is coming from, I like it.

8

It's morning and I'm lying on my back, staring at the bare plywood ceiling five feet above my head. I'm in the top bunk of a fairly uncomfortable double-decker bed. Dr. Clark and my dad slept on cots. My mom and Aimee share a bunk bed across the room. Mira is sleeping below me. I've been lying here all night, thinking about the people in the tavern, about the bartender calling me Ull, about what the day will bring. For the second night in a row, I spent the last eight hours with my eyes open. *How many hours have I been awake?* I wonder.

"Forty-eight," I say to myself.

I've had trouble sleeping before, but nothing like this. And it's not even my horrible thoughts that are keeping me awake. I'm simply not tired.

I slide out of my sleeping bag and dangle my feet over the

edge. My mom is wrapped up in her sleeping bag, still wearing her parka. Aimee too. Dad is buried beneath his blankets. I have no idea what he's wearing. Dr. Clark is sound asleep. Looks to be dressed in a thick sweater. I look down at my legs. I'm wearing sweatpants and a t-shirt. I shed my outer layers last night. I wasn't hot, just itchy.

I should get dressed before Mom sees me, I think. She wouldn't be happy to see me dressed like this. And I don't want her to know I'm not cold. She'd probably think I had a tumor and catch the next flight home. Since it hasn't come up, I don't think Dr. Clark has told my parents yet. He probably knows they'd send me home, too. Besides, if they can keep secrets from me for thirteen years, I'm entitled to keep a few of my own.

I can't see Mira, but I know she's asleep because she snores. They *all* snore. Even if I was tired, I doubt I'd have slept through the noise, any more than I could sleep with a pack of squealing pigs.

The ladder leading to my top bunk squeaks like a tortured lab rat. Using it will only wake everyone up. Without thinking I push off the bed and fall to the floor. I land on my toes, bend at the knees and stop in a crouching position next to Mira, who has a red-hooded sweatshirt up over her head. The agility and silence of my leap brings a smile to my face.

Like a ninja! I think.

I gather my clothes and tiptoe to the open space by the door. The room's only window is on the door. I can see dirty snow on the ground, a bright blue metal shipping container, and a frozen puddle of something foul that can only be vomit. A sense of frustration builds quickly. This is not the Antarctica I came to see.

Before I know what I'm doing, I'm opening the door and stepping outside. I breathe deep. The air is fresh. The sun, just peeking over the horizon, makes me smile. But it's not enough. I need to—

A hand on my shoulder startles me.

Dr. Clark steps around me, fully dressed for frigid conditions, but still hopping up and down, rubbing his arms. Steam pours from his nose and mouth with each breath. I exhale hard and see nothing. Dr. Clark notices, too, but says nothing about it.

"Spoke to a few people last night," he says. "Seems you're something of a legend around here. More than a few stories about your birth have been shared around the fire on cold nights over the past thirteen years. And there are a *lot* of cold nights here. A few people—the ones with functioning brains—are happy to see you back. The others, not so much. If we weren't heading out to Clark Station Two today, we might even have trouble on our hands."

I've heard everything he said, but the only thing that really registers is 'Clark Station Two'. Before I can ask about it, Dr. Clark continues.

He steps in close. "The point is, put on some clothes." He shoves a jacket into my hands. "If anyone saw you out here like this, like it's the middle of the summer, there would be no doubting the stories of your birth."

"I thought I should be proud of being strange," I say, sounding a bit more obtuse than I meant to.

Dr. Clark looks both ways quickly like we're dealing drugs. "Not. Here. People disappear all the time on Antarctica and no one questions why. People get lost in whiteouts. Drunks get buried in snow. It happens. If these people decide a sneeze from you could sever this ice shelf and carry them all into the ocean..."

He doesn't have to finish. I know what he's saying. *I* could disappear.

"You would find me," I say.

He takes my shoulders in his hands. "Solomon, listen. When people go missing in Antarctica, they're usually not found. If they are, they're frozen solid."

"But that can't happen to me."

His voice gets louder. "You'll be as stiff as the rest of them if you've got a knife in your back."

This gets my attention. I'm looking both ways now, too.

"You're changing. We both know it. I saw you jump down from the bed just now. You didn't make a sound. You were in complete control of your body."

This fills me with pride.

"I also saw you fall at my house. I'd never seen a more clumsy kid."

This turns my eyes to the ground. "Why didn't you say anything?"

"I didn't want you to be embarrassed, but if I have to embarrass you now to keep you alive, I will."

I nod, convinced.

But too late. I sense movement to the side. I suck in a panicked breath and turn. But Dr. Clark has sensed it too. He steps closer, obscuring my body with his. He pulls open the door and shoves me inside. The door slams shut as I fall to the floor. I land in a heap, still holding my clothes and the coat Dr. Clark gave me. I look up into the eyes of my mother, father, Aimee and Mira. The way they're looking at me, like I've just stepped out of a flying saucer, tells me everything Dr. Clark said is true.

I start shaking like I'm freezing. "I—I forgot where I was," I say. "Went outside."

My father shakes his head and pulls me to my feet. "That's our Schwartz."

Not any more, I think.

9

The ride to Clark Station Two is long. Nearly two hundred miles. We're traveling at a steady twenty miles per hour. If we don't stop we'll make it there in ten hours, and that's assuming there are no mountains or fissures in the way. That's a full day's drive in a cramped Sno-Cat cabin. There are four cats in our train, each carrying people and supplies. Each is driven by a member of Clark's research team, who arrived a month earlier to oversee the construction of Clark Station Two. Dr. Clark said, "They're the brawn to our brains." I like that—*our* brains. The woman behind the wheel of my Cat is named Collette. She has the same hourglass figure as my mom, but is twice as thick and nearly a foot taller. She's also twice as loud and likes to tell jokes I'm certain my parents wouldn't appreciate.

But my parents aren't here. They're in one of the other Cats catching up with an old friend named Steve Wright. Seems he was part of the original expedition too, but like my parents and the Clarks, had a child—a son named for his father—and hasn't been back since. Steve said he didn't invite his son along because he felt the trip would be too dangerous but then quickly explained that his son was something of a risk taker. "He'd get himself killed on this continent," the man said.

My thoughts drift to the real reason behind our visit to Antarctica, revealed to me just before our Sno-Cat journey began. Clark Station Two was built for the express purpose of an anthropological excavation about a mile from Clark Station One.

Before being forced to abandon Clark Station One, Dr. Clark had found what he believed was the remnants of an ancient wall protruding from the ice. It could turn out to be a random pile of stones, but Dr. Clark felt certain there was more to it. And if he was right...if he was right it would redefine the way we think about the world. A human civilization would have lived on Antarctica before it was frozen over, perhaps before the continent was located at the South Pole. What excited me most about this idea was that it would mean I really did have some kind of geographic ancestry—that I wasn't the first and only Antarctican. The idea fascinated me, and I hoped Dr. Clark would make the discovery during the month my family would be part of the team. *A month is hardly enough time*, I think. I'd prefer to stay here for much longer, maybe forever, continuing Dr. Clark's work.

A loud laugh from Collette snaps me out of my reverie.

Sitting next to the jovial woman is Mira. She's in the front seat, so there won't be any toe touching going on, but I now find her to be a calming presence. In fact, I'm looking forward to exploring and documenting our discoveries together.

Actually, the closer we get to Clark Station Two, the calmer I get. My eyes close a few times, but I don't want to miss the views. I force myself up into a sitting position. Collette has finished her newest joke, something about a horse, and it must have been especially rude because Mira is just smiling uncomfortably.

This seems like a good time to change the subject, so I ask, "How far is the new Clark Station from the first one?"

Collette gives a quick half turn of her head, looking back at me like she forgot I was here. "The boy speaks!"

Now that she mentions it, I realize I haven't really said much of anything in the past three hours. Not that she's given anyone a chance to speak. But I don't recall laughing at her jokes, either.

When she realizes I'm not going to take the bait and offer myself up for teasing, she asks, "What's your interest in the first Clark Station? It's nothing but a sheet of white, just like the rest of this frozen desert."

Despite my doubts about Collette's intelligence, she has accurately described the climate here. The bitter cold saps all the moisture out of the air, turning it into snow or ice. This makes it one of the driest environments on Earth. And the coldest.

I see Mira about to reply and cut her off. "Just curious." I can tell Collette has no knowledge of my birth or the strange events surrounding it. If the story has been kept from new additions to the crew, it must have been at Dr. Clark's request. And he'd been right about keeping it quiet. "My parents worked there," I add.

Mira is squinting at me, but then seems to understand. "My dad did, too...obviously, I guess."

Collette gives Mira a look like she's a pitiful wet cat. "Really," she says, her voice oozing sarcasm.

I'm starting to not like Collette, but I press her for information. "So you haven't been there?"

"I've been there, all right. Clark Station Two is only about five miles beyond Clark Station One. I've driven over the site more than a dozen times. Like I said, nothing but snow. Ain't nothing left."

"Nothing at all?" I say.

"Unless you're some kind of physicist who can see things no one else can."

"Well, we already knew *you* weren't a physicist," I say, immediately wondering if she'll take insult at the comment. The look of horror on Mira's face supports this concern.

But the thick woman guffaws. She holds up her hand. It's hard to see as we bounce over a series of ice heaves, but the one detail I'm sure she wants me to see is hard to miss. Her hand is covered in grime and a layer of black sludge is trapped beneath her fingernails.

"A mechanic," I say.

"Damn straight," she replies, and then launches into a joke about blond mechanics.

I tune her out, thinking about what she said. But my exhaustion suddenly catches up with me. I feel myself lolling over like I've been drugged. I hear Collette's loud voice fade like she's walking away. Then nothing.

I dream of a jungle. It's tropical and lush. The animal calls are like nothing I've heard before. Life surrounds me. I can't see it, but I can sense it. Living, beating hearts. They're getting closer. Hunting me. I long for home, for safety, but don't know the way. The branches scratch me as I run, snagging my clothes, tearing my skin. The cries get louder. Closer. I feel heat on my neck. Something inside me changes with that heat. A sudden rage that spins me around to face my attackers. But I'm alone. That's when I see it—a long gray building, like an airplane hangar. I recognize it immediately.

I sit up, eyes wide. Awake. Collette is quiet now. Mira is staring out the window. A rising panic grips me. We're going to miss it! "Stop the Cat," I say.

Collette snaps to attention, "We're only a few miles away. If you have to pee, you can hold it."

"I need to get out," I say, my voice gravelly with either sleep or anger. I can't tell which.

"Just let him out," Mira says.

"Look, kid, I know that—"

"I'm going to throw up!" I shout. It's a lie, but it gets the desired effect. Collette the mechanic would no doubt be in charge of detailing my lunch from the back seat. The Cat rumbles to a stop. I fling open the door with the desperation of someone who is truly about to puke. I jump to the ice, thrilled to be on my feet again, and run.

I don't know exactly where I'm running, only that I'm drawn forward. I'm focused on the ice, but feel my gaze drawn upward.

There are mountains in the distance. The sight of them stops me in my tracks. I've seen them before. Not just the range, but these exact mountains from a slightly—what should be imperceptible—different angle. About fifteen feet below.

I waste no time thinking about how I can sense the difference in angle. No one is that smart. Not even me. Instead, I fall to my knees and with bare hands, dig into the packed snow. I still can't feel the cold, but I can feel pain. At first, my fingers sting, then they throb. I see streaks of blood in the hard snow, but don't stop. I'm almost there, I'm almost—

A hand on my shoulder stops me. I turn to see my father looking down at me with worried eyes. "What are you doing?"

I'm breathing heavily. And I don't have an answer.

"Where's your coat?" he asks next. But then he's looking beyond me, at the hole I dug. He takes a step back and I see the rest of our crew gathered around in a semi-circle, looking at the boy with no coat and bloody fingers. But my father's not looking at me. I trace his line of vision back to my freshly dug hole and see a gray aberration just beneath the surface.

He kneels down and wipes the snow away. The metal surface is ribbed and slightly curved. He looks at me. "Is this?"

I nod. "Where I was born."

I hear Collette asking "How did he know?" over and over.

"Sol, you shouldn't—"

Something about the tone of his voice coupled with a surge of embarrassment sets me off. "Shouldn't what!" I stand and face him, unleashing years of frustration over my hidden past. "You're the one who hid this from me! You're the one keeping secrets!"

To my surprise, and my father's, I shove him. Hard.

He stumbles back. "Sol..."

I step toward him, bloody fists clenched. Collette is shouting something, her voice warbling like an injured turkey's. I hear my mother's voice, but not her words. "I opened your safe. I found the rock. Why didn't you tell me what would happen."

"What happened?" my father asks.

"Why didn't you tell me?" I shout again. The people standing around me become blurs. I can't see anyone through my tears. My energy drains suddenly and I fall to my knees. The world turns black.

As I fall, my father catches me and picks me up like I'm five years old again. I can feel him carry me back toward his Sno-Cat. I'm asleep before we get there and have no memory of the rest of the trip to Clark Station Two.

10

I wake up confused, not because I don't remember where I am—I know exactly where I am—but because the noise of the place is unfamiliar. I feel like I'm in a subway station and somewhere in the dark, there's a train barreling toward me. Shaking metal. Screeching. A deep resonating rumble that chatters the teeth.

But there is no train. I'm in a bed. There's a wool blanket pulled up to my chin, but it's not itchy. The room is small and formed from four metal walls and a metal ceiling. I've seen bread boxes with more style. There are no windows. A desk with a lamp on top is next to the bed. The lamp is the room's only source of light, glowing a dull yellow.

A rumble rolls across the ceiling, like a wave of energy has coursed through it. Fear twists my gut. Is this my fault? Has the ice broken? I jump out of bed, steadying myself on the desk.

Stumbling toward the door, I notice I'm fully dressed. I'm not wearing a coat, but I've got on insulated pants, full body long johns, a turtleneck and a sweater. I twist the door handle and give it a pull. The door opens and I hear a gentle ring somewhere, but don't bother trying to figure it out. I need to find out what's...happening.

I stop in the hallway and listen. I hear nothing. No storm. No shrieking metal. No subway car. The world has gone silent.

The hallway is long and lined with doors on either side like a college dorm. I'm sure my parents are behind one of these doors, but don't want to risk walking in on a half-dressed Collette or someone else I have yet to meet. I find my feet and walk down the hall, careful not to make any noise.

The hall opens up to a large room that is one part kitchen, one part lounge. Lights triggered by motion sensors illuminate the room. There's a counter-top, sink and fridge to my left; a TV and two couches to my right. A laptop sits closed on a desk. There's a door directly across from the hallway. I head toward it, not knowing what's on the other side.

The door is heavy and thick, but swings open with little effort. The short hallway beyond is lined with jackets and snow gear hanging from hooks. Each set of clothing is labeled with a name. I see mine down near the end.

I pause in front of my jacket, knowing it's not necessary, but consider wearing it anyway. *No*, I think, *it will just get in the way.*

Get in the way of what?

The door leading outside opens just as easily as the first door. I step out into the night and am dazzled by the stars above me. I'm not sure I've ever seen so many, even in the back woods of Maine. But there is an aberration in the sky. One of the stars is moving. It grows closer and I can focus on it, seeing it for its true self—a snowflake lit by the light pouring from the hallway behind me. I've left the door open.

I turn to close the door and notice the sky behind me. There are no stars. Every pinpoint of light in the sky to the south has been blotted out by something massive. *The snowflake*, I think.

That's when I hear it. A tiny *tick*, like a grain of sand falling on a tile floor. I close my eyes and hold my breath. A moment of silence passes before I hear it again. *Tick*. Then again. *Tick, tick.*

It's the snow. I can hear each flake as it lands on the ice.

I smile at the magic of it, of my home, and know I won't be sleeping for the rest of the night. *This is what I came for*, I think. I want to experience this new world and up until this moment, I haven't really. I've made a fool of myself. I've been feared. Maybe even threatened. And I've freaked out almost everyone I've met. Not that everything has been all bad. I consider all the Clarks to be my friends. Dr. Clark is a confidant and mentor. Aimee is a friend and emotional support. And Mira, well she might be all of the above and something more. I'm not sure how teenage courtship is done, but since I'm the only teenage boy within a three thousand mile radius, I think my chances are pretty good. Probably won't be this good ever again.

Carpe diem, Schwartz, I think. *Carpe diem.*

I sense a presence behind me, but unlike so many other times in the past, I'm not frightened. I remember the jingling bell I heard. Dr. Clark no doubt rigged my door so the bell would sound when I left the room. Can't have me walking around in the snow, can we?

I stand there, looking at the stars, waiting for him to give me a coat or tell me to go inside. But he does nothing. *Must be looking at the stars, too,* I think. This late at night, he must figure that no one will see me.

The tick, tick of the falling snow has picked up. "There's a storm coming," I say.

"You have no idea," replies my visitor, but it's not Dr. Clark. The voice is higher and wet.

I turn toward the voice, still not fearing it, then quickly realize I should. A flash of something red, hair maybe, and a streak of dirty flesh is all I see before something strikes me in the stomach and sends me sprawling back onto the ice. I climb to my knees, but the air has been knocked from my lungs. I suck in a breath, but all I manage is a wheeze.

The man laughs at me from the darkness. I can see the door ten feet away, but my attacker has disappeared into the night. I spin around, looking for him, knowing he's going to attack again. But he's invisible, he's—behind me!

I duck low to the ground in a crouch, pivot around and lunge. I throw a punch that feels wild, but the solid impact I feel on my hand tells me I found my target. I see a large shape fall to the snow and pounce on it. One hand has a fist full of fabric, pulling the immobile form up. The other is raised high, ready to strike again.

I let out a roar that sounds something like an angry ape. Then

I see her face.

Her face.

Aimee's face.

The hatch opens and Dr. Clark's silhouette fills the space. "Aimee!" he shouts, jumping to her side. As he lifts her head in his hands, I see her face, swelling and bloody. He turns to me. "What happened?"

But I'm speechless. I can't fathom how to explain what happened, or why. I stand there, as frozen as the ice beneath my feet and for the first time since setting foot on Antarctica, I feel cold. Not my skin. My heart.

Dr. Clark's eyes drift from mine to my clenched fist. He squints at it for a moment and then his eyes are wide and full of fear. He scoops Aimee up and carries her inside without saying another word. When he's gone I look at my fist. It's covered in blood.

Aimee's blood.

11

"What happened?"

I've been asked that question twenty-two times by five different people in the past ten minutes. I suppose they keep asking because I have yet to give a good answer. I'm in shock, but mostly I'm worried sick. I just cold-clocked the person who welcomed me into this world with a smile.

The first thing I did after coming back inside was wash the blood off my hand. It wasn't a matter of erasing the evidence. I had no intention of denying the truth...but I didn't fully know the truth, either. Someone was out there. Someone attacked me. But telling them that—well, it will just make me look crazy.

Crazier.

Aimee is lying on a cot in the living area. Dr. Clark and my mother are tending to her. The rest of the crew stands around waiting like sentinels. Mira kneels by her mother's side, her eyes wet and closed. *Is she praying?* I wonder. My father stands behind me, hands on my shoulders, but I'm not sure if he's comforting me or restraining me.

Aimee moans and blinks for a moment, but doesn't regain consciousness. Dr. Clark looks back at me, his face a mix of anger, sympathy and fear. As the rest of the eyes turn toward me I know the question is going to come again. "*What* happened?"

The tone of his voice tells me I better answer this time.

"I'm sorry," I say.

"Don't be sorry," Dr. Clark says. "Be honest."

"I didn't mean to hurt her."

He gives me a long hard stare. "I believe you."

Some of my tension dissolves with those three words. I'm not sure why I assumed they would all treat me like some kind of untrustworthy criminal. They know me.

I take a deep breath and then spill my emotional guts. "There was someone else out there."

Dr. Clark looks skeptical and I know why. He saw the blood on my hand and is wondering if I'm trying cast the blame on someone else. "I'm not saying I didn't do this, I did."

Collette gasps.

"But I didn't know it was Aimee." The next words are hard to say because even I know they sound ridiculous. "I was attacked."

"In the middle of the Antarctic night?" Collette asks, her voice steeped in a thick tea of doubt. "Were any of you outside tonight?" she asks the crew.

The universal answer to this question is, "no," of course. Even I know that, and I tell them so. "It wasn't any of you."

"Then who?" someone asks.

I meet Dr. Clark's eyes once again. He seems to understand something unusual happened outside. For a moment, I think he's trying to tell me not to speak, but write his expression off to confusion. "It was a man," I say. "I think he had red hair. Long red hair. Maybe closer to maroon. And...and I'm not sure he was wearing clothes."

"What a piece of work," Collette says before letting out a laugh that lets me know she's not buying a word of this. But I don't care about what she thinks. I need Dr. Clark to believe me. I need Mira to believe me. And my parents. I can feel my father's grip on my shoulders tightening. His anger is building with the ridiculousness of my story.

"I'm telling the truth," I say, surprised that I'm standing up to the tank-sized woman. "Someone was out there. He punched me. Knocked me down. I thought Aimee was him."

"Solomon..." the doubt in my father's voice stings with betrayal. How could he believe I did this?

I try to shrug away from my father, but he holds me tight. "I've never hit anyone in my life."

"Could'a fooled me," Collette says. "She's out for the count. Might have a concussion."

"Is that true?" I say, a rising panic making me sick to my stomach.

"Most likely," Dr. Clark says.

Before the interrogation can continue, the roof rumbles. I instantly remember the sounds I heard upon waking. I'd assumed it was part of a waking dream, but I've been awake for too long for that to be the case again. I know for sure when I see everyone in the room look up.

One of the crew, a man I haven't met, dashes to the laptop. I can't see the screen, but I'm sure he's checking the weather. My suspicions are confirmed a moment later. "Holy hell. Wind speed is up to seventy miles per hour!"

The roof shakes again. Louder this time. "Eighty miles per hour!"

My dad takes his hands off my shoulders and enters the hallway leading outside. I hear the second door open a moment later and then quickly close. He returns a moment later, covered in snow.

"It's a whiteout," he says. "I couldn't see more than a foot."

"Where'd this come from?" someone asks. "There was nothing on the weather report."

Dr. Clark and I share a glance. We're both wondering the same thing. Is this my fault?

"This is Antarctica, folks," Dr. Clark says. "This is the kind of thing we expect to happen."

The roof shakes so hard I wonder if it's going tear away.

"One forty!" shouts the man at the laptop.

Collette looks whiter than usual, her eyes locked on the roof. "This place wasn't build to hold up to sustained winds of this force. If this keeps up we'll—"

The lights go out.

Someone whispers, "Oh God."

"What happened?"

While the panicked discussion continues, I listen. Beyond the voices and rumbling wind, something is different. It's not a new sound. It's a missing sound. "The generator is off," I say. I'd heard the rumble of the generator when I woke and recognized the sound from our time in Willy Town.

"He's right," Collette says.

"Where is it?" I ask. "Can we get to it?"

"Backside of this building, between here and the lab. Has its own little hut. But no one can go out there right now. Between the snow and wind, you'd wind up frozen and lost in a matter of minutes."

The discussion continues, but within the hushed cacophony of frightened voices I hear the only one that I want to.

"Merrill," Aimee says.

"I'm here," Dr. Clark says. "The power is out."

"Merrill," she repeats. "He was telling the truth."

"What do you mean?"

"Solomon." Her voice is harder to hear as I sneak away in the dark, but I hear my guilt cleared as I enter the hallway. "There was someone else out there."

A flashlight blinks on.

"Hey, stop!" a voice shouts out.

But they're too late to stop me. I'm already outside. I slam the outer hatch shut and walk into the storm. I hear the door open behind me. I'm only ten feet away, but I'm invisible. Through the howling wind I hear my father's shouting voice. I'd like to stop and chew him out for not believing me, for not trusting me, with anything. But there's no time. Without the generator there is no electricity, but there is also no heat. Within the hour those people inside will be popsicles.

I lift my bare hands up to my face where I can see them. The snow melts on contact as it hits me. I can feel the pressure of the wind, the sting of the whipping snowflakes, but not the cold. Having everyone I love freeze to death would be bad enough, but having to stay out here, waiting for rescue with their corpses...who could endure such a thing?

Tracing a hand along the outer wall of the bunk house I move to the back of the building. The snow is already half way to my knees. If it keeps up, Clark Station Two might be buried. I stop in my tracks. This is my fault. The station is going to be buried, just like the first one was! I double my effort, slogging through the snow. If we need to dig ourselves out in the morning, I want the heat running for as long as possible. Maybe we can make the metal building hot enough to melt the snow gathering on it?

I reach the end of the building and follow the wall around to the back. The building containing the generator must be nearby, but I can't see a thing. I follow the back wall, scouring the area for any hints. That's when I notice a stub of black just above the snow-line. I brush away the snow, finding a wire that leads down to the ice. After digging for a minute I find that it leads straight out and away from the bunk house.

I still can't see it. I pause, recalling the stories of people getting lost in the snow, of death and limb amputation. But those people could feel the cold. I can't. I could probably wait out the storm in a swimsuit and be no worse for wear.

I strike out into the snow, aiming myself along an imaginary line. Ten feet from the bunk house, I realize the wire could have turned in a different direction. I could be going the wrong way. If I don't find it within thirty feet I'll turn around and follow my foot prints back. But a quick glance back reveals my foot prints have been filled with snow or swept away by the wind.

There's no turning back, I decide, and continue forward.

A clang rings out as I run into something solid. I hold my head with one hand and reach out with the other. It's a metal wall covered with snow. If I hadn't run into it, I would have never seen it. I follow the wall and find the door latched shut, but not locked.

I fumble around in the dark, looking for the generator. What I'll do when I find it, I have no idea. I'm sure I can figure it out, but blindness will make the task more difficult. As I graze my hand across the wall, it strikes a hard, plastic, cylindrical object. My mind flashes with recognition as it falls to the floor. I bend down, searching for the flashlight. It's at my feet, and happily, still works.

The beam is dim, but it's enough to light the generator. Two things strike me right away. It's unplugged from the circuit board that distributes the power to all the buildings at Clark Station Two. And the power is switched to "off."

This was no accident caused by the storm.

The red haired man. He's still here. He drew me out.

With my heart hammering, I focus on the task at hand. I go to work on the circuit breakers, turning them all off. The plug goes

in next. Then I turn to the generator. It's been running a while so
it's probably already primed. I switch it to "on" and give the cord
a solid yank. The engine roars to life, healthy and strong. Then
I'm back at the circuit breakers. The main goes on first, then one
switch at a time, slowly restoring power to the system.

The last switch belongs to the generator shed itself. When I
flip the switch the interior lights up so bright that I squint. With
my eyes half closed, I barely make out the figure leaping out from
behind the generator. He's definitely naked, or close to it. His
hair is red. His eyes, like mine, are squinted tight as if the light
hurts, but he seems to have no trouble moving because he hits me
a second later.

The snow outside breaks my fall, but once again I have trouble
catching my breath. I expect him to press the attack, but he vanishes into the storm again.

Or has he? I sense something to my side and look for it. All I
see is a wall of snow. But there's a voice hidden in there. "We've
been waiting a long time for you."

For some reason, I don't doubt or question what he says.
"Who are you?"

"I'm who you will become."

A blow to the side of my head sends me sprawling. I think
about the pain and how much it must have hurt Aimee when I
hit her. I roll over and try to sit up, but I'm pinned. I can't see
him, but I know the man is straddling my waist. His face resolves
from the snow. His skin is white, whiter than mine if that's possible, and opaque. Blue veins pulse just beneath the surface. His

eyes are wide now, and dark. Nearly black. His smile reveals shat-
tered and rotting teeth. I can't see his body. It's blocked by snow
and the unnatural blood red dreadlocks dangling from his head.

When he speaks I smell his breath, like rotten ground beef.
But the smell doesn't bother me nearly as much as his words,
"Time to go home."

The pain from the first blow to my head quadruples with the
second. I'm dazed now, nearly unconscious. I feel pressure
around my ankles and a scraping on my back. He's dragging me.
After a few moments, the sky above me begins to clear. The
storm is easing. For a moment I can see the storm overhead. But
then the reality of my situation sets in—I'm being taken—and
the night sky is blurred by my tears.

I hear my name being called in the distance. My father's voice.
Then my mother's. Dr. Clark's. Mira's. They're looking for me.

"Here," I mumble.

Then the silhouette of my captor blots out the sky. I hear my
name one more time, the voice as desperate as I feel. I open my
mouth and fill my lungs to respond, but I never get the chance. I
don't feel the blow. I'm unconscious before the pain registers.

I awake—who knows how much later—and find myself underground.

Covered in blood and surrounded by bodies.

12

My foot rolls on a bone as I kick away from the bodies. There's so many of them, I can't make out what I'm seeing. It's like someone decided to play a game of pick-up sticks with discarded bones. I fall backwards, landing on a lumpy mass. My hands are out, bracing against injury. Rubbery flesh breaks my fall, its coarse hair tickling between my fingers. I haven't seen the body beneath me, but I know—somehow—that it's dead.

Long dead.

This is little comfort, however. After finding my footing, I stand bolt upright. My chest heaves with each breath. Each draw of air is deep, but the oxygen isn't getting to my head. I try breathing through my nose, and the rotten stench of old meat and something worse twists my stomach with the violence of a tornado. I drop to one knee, fighting a dry heave.

"Slow down," I tell myself. "Breathe."

I breathe through my mouth. I can *taste* the foul air, but I force each breath into my lungs, hold it and then let it out slowly. Just like I learned at soccer practice. I only lasted a few practices before giving up, but at least I came away with something. Calm down. Focus. Breathe.

My body settles. I'm no longer shaking. But when I look up I wonder if I've done something wrong. Stars blink in the darkness, like when you stand up too fast. But they're not floating around. They're just tiny points of light, like actual stars, but I get the feeling they're a lot closer. The brightest of the light points are directly behind me, and to test my theory I reach out for them. My hand strikes a solid wall.

Stone.

The points of light are small glowing stones, crystals maybe. I'd be fascinated if I weren't absolutely terrified.

My hand yanks away from the cool surface as though repulsed by a magnetic force. For the first time since waking, a rational thought enters my mind.

Where am I?

It's a simple question. Finding the answer will give me focus. I turn my mind to the task while my body works the adrenaline out of its system.

The dull yellow stars behind me are large, perhaps the size of quarters. They wrap around in both directions, almost vanishing as they shrink with the distance. But I can see them surrounding me with a flow of tiny lights. There is no door. No escape.

I'm in a pit.

Full of bodies.

Long dead bodies, I remind myself as my breathing quickens. It's like looking at the mummies in The Museum of Fine Arts. *They can't hurt you.*

With my eyes better adjusted to the dim light, I crouch down to look at the bone I stepped on. What I see causes me to hold my breath, but I find myself calming down for two reasons. First, my mind is engaged, and like Spock, my emotions, which can overwhelm me, are being choked out. Second, the bones are not human.

The nearest limb looks like a femur, but it's as thick as a cow's and half the length. I try to picture an animal that would have such thick, short limbs, but nothing comes to mind.

I scan the field of bones. Most are similar in thickness and size, but many I can't identify. Whatever these bones belonged to, I'm fairly certain they're not human. In fact, they don't belong to any creature I've ever seen before.

Remembering the soft flesh that broke my fall, I turn around and look down. If not for the clumps of rough red hair sticking out of the sheet of white skin, I might have mistaken it for a chunk of rug padding. The skin is thick, perhaps a half inch, and hasn't decomposed at all despite the bones beneath it being free of flesh.

A scuff above me turns my head up as dirt and dust fall into my face. Someone is above me.

"Who's there?" My voice echoes.

The only response I get is silence, which makes me angry. I've been beaten and kidnapped after all. "Hey! I know you're there!"

"I wouldn't do that if I were you."

The sinister scrape of the voice makes my stomach muscles tighten. This is the man who took me.

"Why?" I ask through clenched teeth, determined not to show this man fear.

"Because..." I suspect his pause is for dramatic effect. When I feel the sudden urge to pee, I know it's working. "...you're not alone."

I spin around, forgetting all about my bladder. I can't see more than ten feet of body-strewn floor. Beyond that it's just a sea of light flecks. If there is someone down here with me, I'll never see them.

Then I do.

In the same way we detect distant objects moving in space, I see a body shifting to my left, blocking out the small lights.

"Who is it?" I whisper.

"Not a who," answers the voice.

Not a who? *Not a who!*

"What am I supposed to do?" My whisper is urgent, hissing like the man's voice.

"Survive. Escape."

"How?"

"That's up to you." I hear him shuffling away from the edge. His voice fades as he speaks for the last time. "I will not see you again until you do."

A rattle of bones turns my attention back to the sneaking shadow. My eyes widen. It's no longer slinking to the side. It's growing larger, blocking out more and more stars. That's when I realize it's not growing larger, it's getting closer.

In the moment before it strikes, I hear it suck in a high pitched whistle of a breath. I duck down to pick up the thick bone that tripped me up. But it's too late. The thing is upon me.

13

I scream.

I'm too terrified to do anything else. My hands are on my head. I'm pitched forward. My eyes are clenched shut. Every muscle in my body has gone tight, as though clutched in rigor.

It knocks me back and I spill into a pile of bones and old skin. But I feel no weight on top of me. No gnashing of teeth on my body. The thing has missed its tackle, striking a glancing blow as it passed, but nothing more. Perhaps because I bent down. Perhaps because it can't see well in the dark. I don't know. I don't care.

I'm alive. For now.

And I don't want to die.

But I'm certain I'm going to and the events of the past few months replay in my mind. I can't stop it. I can't control it. And in a flash, I'm back at the beginning. A moment later, my mind returns to the present. I'm still in the pit. Still waiting for death. But I feel different somehow.

My attention is drawn down. The thick bone is still in my hand. I stand, holding it at the ready like Hercules's club or Thor's hammer. What I wouldn't give for an ounce of their strength right now.

But strength is something I lack. I can already feel my limbs growing weak from fright. If this fight doesn't end quickly I'll probably lie down and accept death like a deer in the jaws of a mountain lion. It always amazes me how quickly prey animals accept their fate once caught. Will I be any different?

The answer surprises me.

A shift of shadow to my left catches my eye. But this time the fear is drowned out by a rage I have felt before, a rage that now has an outlet. I lunge for the shadow, bone-club raised. The thing flinches back, surprised by my attack. My first swing misses, nearly spinning me around. But I follow it up with a backhand swing worthy of John McEnroe. The impact hurts my arm, but it lets me know I've hurt the thing, too.

The thing stumbles back, letting out a high pitched whine as it strikes the wall. I struggle to see it, but it's backlit by the wall. I can, however, see its silhouette more clearly now. Its body is egg-shaped and maybe four feet tall, with short, thick legs. Its arms are almost comical—short stubs sticking out to either side as useless as a T-Rex's tiny appendages. I feel emboldened by the thing's size and awkward build. But I've underestimated its will to live. This thing doesn't want to die as much as I don't.

It lets out a shrill scream and charges again. I start to duck, but this time it doesn't leap. Instead, it lowers its top half—I can't see where the head begins or ends or if it even has a head—and plows into me like a battering ram. It lifts me off the ground and carries me ten feet before slamming me into a stone wall. I hear a crack as my head strikes, but I don't lose consciousness. There's too much adrenaline in my system for that to happen.

But when I open my eyes and look at the thing, I wish I had fallen unconscious. Then I wouldn't have seen it. I wouldn't be awake when it devoured me. But I am awake, staring into a set of jaws that looks like it belongs to a great white shark—rows of serrated triangular teeth set into a jaw that protrudes from the mouth. The entire top half of the creature, just above its pitiful arms, has opened up to take me in. I have no doubt I'll be severed in half. I'll spend my last living moments bleeding out in this thing's gullet.

I can't die like this.

"Get off of me!" I scream. My voice distracts the creature. Its jaws close slightly, revealing a pair of perfectly black eyes, like two eight balls jammed into the top of a killer Humpty Dumpty. Tufts of thick brown hair cover its milky skin.

I've seen this before. The remains of these creatures litter the cave floor. These things aren't killing people here, they're being killed. It wasn't put here to kill me, I was put here to kill *it*.

"Get off me, I said!" I shout, further confusing the beast. I dive to the side, but it clamps down on my shirt—a red, white and blue flannel that looks much more patriotic than any piece of clothing should. I spin around and lose my balance. The shirt rips as I fall away. My hands stretch out to brace my fall and I plunge into a litter of bones—the bones of this thing's kin. But my right hand catches on something sharp. A hot burn strikes my palm, followed by a warm gush of liquid over my wrist.

I'm bleeding.

And the thing can smell it. I hear its quick breaths, sniffing as a dog does. Then I hear the smacking of lips and then it moves again, closing in on me.

Ignoring the pain in my hand, I dig into bones and find the sharp object. Playing my fingers over it gently, I feel a large triangular tooth. Then another. And another. In my mind's eye I can see its shape: a broken jawbone from one of these creatures. I find an end that has no teeth and grip it.

I'm back on my feet for only a moment before the creature charges again. But I'm ready for it. Whatever this thing is, it's deadly, but it's not smart enough to realize I would anticipate the same attack.

I step to the side and swing down. I feel an impact, and then a tug on my weapon as the teeth catch flesh. A sound like tearing paper fills the air and makes me sick to my stomach. I can't see it, but I know I have just sliced open the creature's back.

It whimpers and stops.

I step closer.

It steps away.

Some instinct I never knew I had tells me I've inflicted a mortal wound. The thing is dying. I see its form again as it nears the far wall—egg shaped body, tiny arms, squat legs, large eyes. And I recognize it for what it is. Not the species, the age.

It's a baby.

I've just killed a baby.

As it mewls against the wall, each call weaker then the last, the jaw-weapon falls from my hand.

"No," I whisper, falling to my knees. What kind of a sick world have I been brought to?

I want my mother.

I scream for her. "Mom!" I scream again and again, my voice growing hoarse. My face is wet with tears and snot. My body is wracked by sobs between each shout for my mother. My thoughts turn to my father. How awful he must feel now that I'm gone, knowing I disappeared while angry with him. Not only had he lied to me for thirteen years, but he also believed I was capable of hurting Aimee. He didn't trust me. Never had. But I trusted him now. *Was this what he was protecting me from?* This thought strikes me like a fist and I long for my father's presence. He could protect me. I yell for him next.

But he doesn't come. He can't hear me. He'll never hear me again. How could he?

My voice fades to a whisper. Pain stabs my head with every beat of my heart. The pinpricks of light surrounding me are now blurry halos. In the quiet, I can no longer hear the ragged breathing of the young creature. Certain it's dead, I weep again, mourning not just the death of this deformed thing that tried to eat me, but the death of something much more precious to me:

my soul. As my body gives way to exhaustion, I slide down onto the stone floor, surrounded by bones and wonder, *maybe that's the point.*

14

Three days have passed. At least I think it's been three days. Feels like it anyway. But there really is no time down here. And my watch is missing, so I have no way to measure time other than to count it out in my head. But that kind of concentration is impossible with my stomach growling. That's too mild a word. It feels like a rabid hamster with razor claws is loose in my gut. I'm being eaten alive from the inside out. My already skinny frame has lost several pounds.

But that's not the worst of it. People can go without food for a good number of days, but not water. Three days is the max. I'm still alive because I haven't sweated, I haven't moved much at all. I considered drinking my own urine—it *is* sterile—but couldn't bring myself to do it. I now regret that decision. My lips are starting to crack. My tongue is swollen and I feel a relentless fatigue.

I'm never going to get out of here.

Even if I were healthy, I couldn't escape.

I checked all the walls; they're fifteen feet tall all around. There are a few crevices and centimeter deep ledges that I'm sure a rock climber could use to scale toward freedom. But I'm a thirteen-year-old bookworm. I have trouble climbing the staircase at the Bunker Hill Monument in Boston. At my best I would be trapped here, and I'm currently at my worst, or quickly nearing it.

For a moment, I wish Justin were here with me. He's the consummate preteen boy. MVP of the soccer team I quit. Manages trees like a monkey. I'm sure his ancestors were successful hunter-gatherers. Sure, my ancestors might have discovered fire or invented the wheel, but in a pit of doom I'd take his lineage any day. He'd have climbed out of this pit before the egg monster emerged from the shadows.

And I am seeing shadows now. Over the past three days my eyes have adjusted to the darkness more than I thought possible. I can see the walls of the pit around me, lit by the crystals. It's still not quite enough to read by—not that I have a book—but seeing provides at least some comfort.

Thinking of Justin makes me homesick. I'm sure my parents are still searching for me. I'm sure Dr. Clark has told them about my inability to feel cold here. They still have hope. But I'm so far away.

Of course, this cavern could be only ten feet below Clark Station Two. It's impossible to tell, but I feel a distance from the world that I can't explain. I'm trapped in a dream. Or on another planet. Beyond reach.

In my heart I know it's true. At the very least I'm out of earshot. I screamed my voice raw earlier. I don't know if my throat has healed yet. I haven't tried speaking. There's no one to talk to, and I'm determined not to go mad talking to myself. What would a crazy person do down here? There are no pigeons to feed.

A smell tickles my nose.

The hamster in my stomach runs circles.

I smell meat. Cooking meat.

I don't recognize it, but I would eat it. I would devour it.

I stand, fighting the ache in my legs, and smell the air. It's divine. I wait there and count out ten minutes, hoping my captor doesn't want me to die. *He'll bring me food*, I tell myself. *He needs me for something. He wants me to survive.*

On my own.

The thought is mine, but I fight against it. There is no arguing, though. He wants me to survive. To escape, even. But without help. This is some kind of test. Like when I met Justin. After his mother escorted him to my backyard and asked if I would play with him, I brought him to a neighbor's yard and had him scale a fifteen foot hunk of granite. I couldn't do it myself, but he didn't know that. I was in awe when he did it. And he was in awe at what I could do with LEGOs. It was a simple test: complete this task and we will be friends. Could this be something similar?

The hamster is in a rage. "Eat!" it shouts from within.

"Eat what?" I say aloud.

My voice is apparently healed.

As I spin around, looking for a meal that isn't there, I see the limp silhouette of the egg-monster.

No, I think, but my legs are already carrying me toward it.

Before I see the thing, I smell it. The odor of decomposition turns my stomach, gagging the hamster momentarily. But then it returns, stronger then ever.

I reach out for the beast, regardless. Its flesh is rubbery and rough. I push, mouth watering with the expectation of feeling firm, potentially edible muscle. But the body gives like a water balloon. I wonder if its insides have liquefied, decomposing fully within itself in just three days. I confirm this theory when I push on the skin, and a thick black gel oozes from the wound I created. The substance slides slowly and then slips free, falling onto the back of my hand.

I yank back from it, disgusted. The smell hits me again, but this time it's not the body that stinks—I've backed ten feet away—it's my hand that reeks. I shake it, flinging the rotten jelly to the floor, coating stone and old bone alike. But I can't remove it all. I take off my shirt, wipe my hand clean and wind up to throw the shirt to the top of the fifteen foot wall.

As the shirt flies away from me, I think better of discarding it and pinch the fabric just in time. I hold it out away from me and then discard it on the opposite end of the pit.

When I'm done, I'm struck by the fact that I'm back to square one.

The hamster is picking up speed.

The odor of cooking meat grows stronger.

Weakness washes over me.

But then something new joins the chorus of discomfort. A sound.

In all my time here, the only thing I've heard is myself. My breathing. My voice. My movements. Other than that, this place is more silent than anything I've ever experienced. So the wet slurp I hear now strikes my ears like a gunshot.

I spin, looking for the source, and find nothing. There is nothing around me, in the pit or atop the wall. The floor is stone.

Up, my subconscious whispers. *Look up.*

I have yet to see the ceiling of the cave. It is the one place that remains concealed by absolute darkness. But now something descends from above. It reminds me of an oversized drop of honey, pushed slowly from the bottle and stretching out. A giant teardrop.

But this does not look sweet. Slime drips from its sides. I can't see its true color, but my imagination colors it mucus green. And it's wriggling. From the inside. As it dangles just above the floor, I step closer.

Something moves within. I see the shape first, bulbous and stubby. Through the translucent skin I see distorted details—mottled flesh, a wide, sickly grinning mouth and closed eyes.

The two large eyes snap open. Black circles stare back at me. Only a foot of open space and a lettuce-thin sack separate the newly birthed egg-monster and me. It sees this just as easily as I do, and like me, it is hungry.

Its stubby arms claw at the sack, tearing it with small, but sharp claws. It's like a giant sized clone of the hamster in my stomach.

That's not entirely true. The hamster is on my side. And it, too, is clawing to get out.

As I turn and run, I know this fight will be different. The outcome may change. I may lose my life. But this time...this time we won't just be trying to kill each other, we'll be trying to eat each other.

I pick up my tooth-filled jawbone and spin around, facing the creature as it emerges from its womb.

15

My first mistake is assuming that this creature will act and react like the first. It doesn't. While the first egg-monster charged like a bull, this one is intent on dizzying me. It runs in frantic circles, spiraling slowly toward me with each lap. A thick glob of drool stretches from its open, dagger-filled mouth. I'm positive it will switch directions at any moment, and by the time it does, I'll probably be on the floor watching the room spin.

My second mistake is over-estimating my own abilities. The thing has been sprinting madly for only thirty seconds, but the jaw-saw (that's what I'm calling my weapon) already feels heavy in my hand. My heart pounds from exertion and fear. I stumble around on weak legs, tracking its run.

I can't keep it up. I've got maybe a minute of energy left. Probably less before I succumb to dizziness.

So I stop and catch my breath.

This seems to confuse the creature. Its next two circles maintain a ten foot radius.

I watch it run as my dizziness ebbs. Its stubby legs are ridiculous. To say the egg-monster is running isn't accurate. Bobble's the word. The ten-inch legs, which end in small two-digit feet, have no knees. Each step brings the leg out and around. Like I said, ridiculous.

Then it's moving closer again. Only now I know exactly where it's going to strike. I think I've got it outsmarted, and perhaps I did at one point, but I've already repeated mistake number two.

It lunges from behind, as expected, and I spin to greet it, raising the jaw-saw and swinging. But the weapon is heavy and my movement is at half speed. Rather than striking the beast with a row of razor sharp teeth, I biff it dully with my forearms.

My only consolation is that the movement saved my life. Rather than ending up inside the gaping shark-like jaws, it sideswipes me and sends me sprawling. The rough skin of the creature rubs against my arms as it passes, sheering off a few layers of my skin. But I hardly notice the burn. There is no time to consider it. The creature is arcing into another spiraling sprint.

I regain my feet, holding my weapon in both hands. It's going to wear me down. Just standing now is a challenge.

Then it occurs to me that even though this creature has a different plan of attack than the first, it may be equally dull. *It will try the same thing again.* I'm sure of it. It will run circles, close in and then pounce from behind. Probably from the same optimal distance. Not that any of that will help me. I still won't be able to spin and strike.

So I'll just have to stop it before it gets that far.

I judge the distance between us.

Five rotations left.

I grip the jaw-saw like a baseball bat. I haven't played since T-ball, but I remember the basics. Eye on the ball. Step into the swing. Follow through.

When it begins its fifth and final revolution, it passes within range. I shout, step forward and swing with all my remaining strength, which isn't much, but I'm swinging into its run. Its own momentum should inflict most of the damage, I just need to get the jaw-saw there.

The blow is solid and sends a tingle up my arms. The jaw-saw is yanked from my hand. I turn to watch it go, hoping to see its teeth buried inside the beast. But they're not. The egg-monster's jaws have clamped down on my weapon.

The thing stops and gives the object in its mouth a few playful tosses, like a dog with a dead mouse, positioning my weapon across its own jaws. It turns to me, its black spherical eyes somehow conveying humor. Then it bites down. The jaw-saw shatters into three fragments. The two on the sides of its mouth spin away onto the bone littered floor. A giant black tongue pushes the third piece from its mouth, then works at the tiny fragments encased in its drool.

One bite, I think. *That's all it will take. One bite and I'm lunch.*

I back away, but don't watch my step. A bone trips me and sends me to the floor. As I scramble away on my hands and feet, the thing rises taller. Seeing me on my back triggers something in the creature. It knows I'm defenseless.

Flinging its short, straight legs into motion, the thing charges. Now it's acting like its sibling. But it's faster. More ferocious. It occurs to me, as the thing bears down on me, that the first egg-monster I faced had already been in the pit for who knows how long. It was already weakened. I think this one could fight all day without stopping.

Not that it will have to. The fight will be over in ten seconds—the time it will take it to reach me.

I reach out with my hands, searching for something with which to defend myself. My right hand grasps a long bone. I pull it out. It's a human femur. I nearly drop it in disgust, but manage to hold onto it and thrust it out, hoping to channel Luke Sky-walker's Rancor-stopping technique.

In a flash I see the bone I'm holding enter the creature's open maw. Then the jaws close. My eyes close, too, so I don't see what happens next. But I hear it. And then feel it. A crunch and slurp of splitting flesh strikes my ears a moment before an intense pain jolts up my arm.

I scream as I'm struck and lifted. A moment later the back of my body and head strikes the solid wall of the pit. Spots of light dance in my vision for a moment and then fade. I wait for a second strike, for teeth to surround and sever my head.

But the attack has stopped. The pressure holding me against the wall is steady. The egg-monster has stopped moving. And then I see why.

The broken bone I jabbed into the creature's mouth ended with a jagged, sharp tip. The creature's own powerful jaws had shoved the bone up through its head and out its forehead. I can only assume it pierced whatever passed for a brain in the process.

But before it died, the beast's jaws did their work, closing just enough to grip my arm in a death-vise. It could be worse. The bite could have easily severed the limb. The four quarter-inch-deep puncture wounds are insignificant by comparison. Of course, there is still the issue of freeing my arm from the jaws without filleting my skin.

The creature is heavy and hard to push, but it's still on its feet, and once propped up, begins to fall backward, which is extremely painful for me since my arm is still clutched in its jaws. I move with it, hopping up onto its body, straddling it just below the lower jaw. The movement deepens the wounds and sends a fresh wash of pain through my body. I grunt, which sounds more like a primitive growl, and steady myself above the creature.

Its black eyes have fogged over. The black tongue dangles from the side of its partially opened mouth. My blood seeps over the gleaming white teeth and drips into the thing's throat. For a moment I fear it will awaken and finish the job, but then I look again at the large bone sticking out of its head.

"You're dead," I tell it.

But it doesn't reply.

"I'm going crazy," I say. "But you? You're dead."

I plant my right foot against its upper jaw and push down. For a moment it doesn't budge, but then slowly, the jaws separate. I was hoping the mouth would simply snap open and get the painful part over with, but no such luck. I can feel the teeth sliding slowly out of my flesh. A warm pulse of blood pours out. A snag and pull of serrated tooth on sinew follows, along with a stab of pain. The thirty seconds it takes to free my arm feels like thirty minutes.

But then I'm free and standing over the monster like Hercules himself. Wounded, but alive.

I stand still for a moment, my chest heaving with each breath. *I'm changing*, I think, and realize I have thought this before. It began when I arrived at Antarctica and I couldn't feel the cold. My agility increased. Then my confidence. And now some hidden killer instinct has emerged. I'm not sure what this is, but it's helping me adapt, physically and emotionally, to this harsh new life. So I'm thankful for it.

I look at my wounds. There are four of them. Assessments run through my mind: stitches, antibiotics, apply pressure. But I ignore them. Something else has my attention. The hamster in my gut had hidden while I was fighting for my life, but now that the deed is done and I'm still breathing, it's back with a vengeance.

For a moment I consider finding the shirt I discarded and tying some clean strips around the wound, but now something else distracts me from the injury: a fragment of jaw-saw still holding three teeth. I move back to the carcass and kneel by one of the muscle-filled stubby legs.

My first cut is tentative.

The second goes deep.

By the third I'm lost in my hunger and sawing away.

Moments later, I'm eating.

I'm surviving.

For now. I have no idea what comes next.

16

After filling my belly, I weep.

Not from guilt over the horrors I'd seen and done. Not for the newborn monsters I'd slain, or even the one I'd eaten—I've had veal before and calves are infinitely more adorable than the egg-monsters. I understand survival of the fittest. In school I had been at the bottom of the food chain.

The killing doesn't bother me. I'm far from a vegetarian and these things are hardly animals in my book. It is my unexpected response to these things that revolts me.

I didn't notice at first. But as I cut and eat the flesh, and drink the life-giving blood, I become aware of a tightness in my cheeks. The kind you feel after going to a friend's birthday where wearing a grin is as mandatory as the party hats.

I am smiling.

The meat is stringy and tough. It tastes unlike anything I've had before, but is decidedly raw—firm and slimy, like chunks of a rubber slug. But I am enjoying it. When my self-awareness returns—I don't know when it checked out—I am horrified by what I find.

My t-shirt is blood-stained and beginning to dry. The coagulation clings to my chest. My cheeks and chin are saturated in blood and bits of flesh. I can feel my skin tightening as it dries. With no water to wash myself, I know the red stain will turn brown and flaky, only disappearing when my outer layers of skin fall away.

I see myself without a mirror. Feral and frightening. My hair dangles in front of my wet eyes. The blond hair has turned red at the end. I don't remember getting my hair in the blood, but it *is* long and I don't recall much of anything about my recent meal.

I move to stand and my stomach protests. I'm not sure I've ever eaten more. My gut, normally flat and skinny, is distended, but not from hunger like the Ethiopians on the news. My stomach is full of raw egg-monster. I'm like a lion that gorges and then rests in wait for the next meal.

Unable to move, I realize that's exactly what I need to do, too. I'm not sure how long the carcass will keep. It's cool in the pit, but the other body turned to a jelly filled sack within days. I might get one more meal out of it, but I'm not sure. I need to rest, I decide. And wait.

It was three days between hatchings, maybe four. It may be as many before my next meal arrives.

I feel I should cry again, thinking of these living newborns as meals to be slaughtered, but I don't. It's the way of things now. I have no choice in the matter. My tears dry as I fall asleep.

I dream of darkness.

Not total darkness. I sense a light source behind me and to the sides I see a fading blue. As I fight to move, I realize I'm swimming—clawing at the water. Below me is a face surrounded by a white veil. I close the distance. The veil is hair. The face is Mira's.

I wake up.

Tears return, but I don't embrace them. I stand and kick my foot angrily, stubbing a toe on a loose bone. I pick up the limb and throw it out of the pit. My stomach rumbles through the streams of tears. I'm hungry already? How long did I sleep? I have no way to know.

As I walk to the carcass, my stomach growls with expectation. The hamster has not yet risen, but I can feel him stirring.

I stop short of the slain creature. A puddle of fetid black slime surrounds it. The meat is useless to me. But how long did it take? How much time has passed? Not having all the answers is a new feeling for me and it roils my already fragile emotional state.

More tears come. "Stop crying," I grumble at myself. The new, cold corner of my soul tells me no amount of tears can help me. The logic that I have always embraced tells me I will need the fluids. The recently released animal in me licks the salty tears from my cheeks as they pass—this seems mostly involuntary.

"Stop crying!" I scream. "You weak fool. You pitiful little thing!"

I choke out a single sob and then set my face into a stone-like gaze. The tears built up in my eyes drip free, but no more follow. Something in me has broken, or has been fixed. I suppose that's a matter of perspective.

I vow to never shed a tear again. Not while I'm here. There is no room for those kinds of emotions. They're a weakness. I squelch my sadness, homesickness, compassion and kindness. If they rule me here, I will die.

Free of these things, my thoughts clear and for the first time since waking up in the darkness, I ponder escape. I approach the wall and once again feel the rough, cracked surface. Only this time, I dig my fingers in and pull. To my surprise, I am able to lift myself off the ground. But only for a moment. My fingernails bends backward and I fall to the stone floor. The knob of some discarded limb digs into my leg. I stand and kick it away, ignoring the pain, and return to the wall.

My second attempt is no more successful. I'm not strong enough to climb out, but that can change. My fingernails aren't thick enough, but that too can change. And if it can't, my mind will come up with a solution my body can handle.

A slurping sounds from behind. I recognize it and spring into motion without hesitation. I no longer have the jaw-saw, but any sharp object will work. I pick up a humerus—human—but I'm unfazed by that detail. The knobby head of the bone shatters away when I smash it against the wall, leaving a jagged, but sharp tip behind.

It's a short spear, but it will work.

I turn and see the egg-sack lowering from above. The thing inside has not yet begun moving. And I'm determined to never give it the chance. It goes against my sense of fairness, but my life isn't exactly fair anymore, either. There are no rules here.

I rush the thing silently, knowing a battle-cry might startle it into action. Then I'm in the air, arms back and spring loaded. I thrust the bone forward, piercing the opaque sack and then the egg-monster within. The whole dangling thing shifts when I strike. It stretches out as I pull it to the ground and pin the now writhing creature to the floor. With a loud snap, the stretched material breaks open above my head.

As the broken tendril retracts into the darkness above me, a gush of fluid pours out. It washes over me, but I pay no attention to it. The creature beneath me has stopped moving. And I am hungry.

For a moment, some part of my mind thinks, *I am lost*, but the thought is quickly overwhelmed by, *I am hungry*.

As I tear away the gelatinous womb my smile returns.

This time, I welcome it.

17

Killing. Eating. Sleeping.

That sums up what my life has become. Days and hours have no meaning anymore so I can't say how much time has passed. All I know is that I kill an egg-monster, I eat egg-monster meat to the point of bursting and then I sleep. When I wake, I'm hungry again and it's not long before the next hatchling arrives. This cycle leaves me very little time to focus on escape, and deviating from it could mean death.

I'm not sure how many times the cycle has repeated. I never do try to count. But there are many more bones in the pit than when I arrived.

During the small periods of time I have, mostly while eating, I think about escape. I have tried piling the bones, but the rounded surfaces can't support my weight. I've tried fashioning a rope from strands of the egg monsters' skin, but the flesh never truly dries and the knots binding them slip apart. And despite a thickening of my muscles, I have not yet been able to scale the walls, though I have lost a few fingernails in the effort.

Having just finished a meal, I burp and sit back, thinking about how much sweeter this egg-monster tasted. My father used to say that taste buds change. I always thought he was just saying that to get me to eat something I didn't like, but maybe he was right? I may have acquired the taste for egg-monster steaks.

"Raw, please," I say, grinning.

And no, thinking of my father didn't make me sad. Not at all. As promised, I have not shed a tear.

As I pick my teeth with a bone shard, I see a splash of color peeking out from beneath some bones. It's my shirt. Not my undershirt. I discarded that along with my pants when they became too thick and sticky with blood. This is the patriotic flannel I got rid of because it became fouled by the decomposed remains of an eggy. That hardly bothers me now, but I still feel no cold, so the shirt holds little interest.

As a shirt.

It could be used for something else entirely, I realize.

I can feel the meal making me drowsy. I know eating a lot of turkey doesn't really make people tired. It's the full stomach. And my stomach is certainly full. The effect of eating the egg-meat is like popping a sleeping pill. No matter how hard I fight, I'll be asleep within ten minutes.

I have just enough time to grab the shirt and return to what has become my home—a ten foot radius of floor I keep free of bones and blood. I have lined the floor with the skins of several egg-monsters, and in the middle I have several stacked up. It's nearly as comfortable as my bed back home.

I make it back to my bed with the shirt just in time. Seconds later I'm asleep. The process of waking, killing, eating and sleeping repeats several more times before my latest escape plan comes to fruition. I get a few minutes here and there to shred the fabric, select prime bones—they need to be strong and sharp. Finally I create my bindings and cinch them to my hands.

Having just awakened, I hold my hands up and look at the newly fashioned climbing claws inspired by Justin's Ninja magazines. Eat your heart out, Michael Dudikoff. I have tied a filed down jaw fragment to both hands. Each contains three short, serrated triangular teeth that I've made sure can support my weight. They will do the job my fingernails have failed to do. But I've gone a step further. Atop each first joint knuckle is a longer, thinner tooth. When I make a fist, they stick out a full inch. A punch would inflict four puncture wounds. A swipe would be just deep enough to eviscerate and kill an egg-monster.

There will be no more looking for or losing weapons. I am the weapon now. And with my hands free, I can climb out of here with everything I need, which is nothing. My clothes are gone except for my brown flannel boxers and I tore those up the legs because they occasionally hindered my mobility. I'm sure I look like a teenaged Tarzan, but who's going to see me down here? I got rid of my boots. They were heavy, slowed me down and made climbing all but impossible. My toes grip the stone much better and the soles of my feet have become leather thick. I can also move in silence.

I stare up at the fifteen foot wall and, for a moment, doubt what I'm about to try. Not because I think I'll fail, but because for the first time, I think I'll succeed. I've become comfortable here. The routine is comforting. I'm surviving. Above this wall...I have no idea what awaits me. I could just stay. But my curiosity is a force to be reckoned with and no matter how cold I have become inside, it will always be the force that guides my actions.

I place my hand against the wall, sliding it up until I find a lip with my fingertips. I raise my hand higher until I feel the teeth of my climbing claw slip into place. I repeat the process with my other hand, digging in a little bit higher. One of my feet goes next, finding a crack to wedge in. Then, with all three limbs I heave myself up.

I find a foothold first, then begin the search for the next hand-hold. When I've found it, I start on the other hand.

That's when I hear the slurp.

An egg-monster is descending.

My stomach growls.

My hand pauses.

If my climb fails and I fall back down, the beast will be free and waiting. I consider leaping down and killing the thing before leaving, but I know that if I smell its blood, I will eat. And if I eat, I will sleep. And the will to escape might very well have left me by then. It has to be now. Or I'll spend the rest of my life here.

The thing hits the stone floor with a wet splat. I can hear it tearing through the womb.

For a moment I can taste it and the long-silent hamster comes to life. I'm a slave to this hunger and that fact fills me with anger. I have sacrificed a lot to survive, to reach this point. I will not be a slave to this thing, this cycle.

I close my eyes and take a deep breath. As I reach up to find the next hand-hold, I can hear the monster breathing now. Its awkward legs are stepping in circles. It's hungry too, and no doubt smells my rank scent.

The teeth of my climbing claws bite into the stone and I rise higher. The movement betrays my position. The thing is coming for me and I'm not yet high enough to avoid its jaws.

I block out the oval-shaped human-eating Pac-Man pounding toward me and focus on the wall. I move with confidence, pushing and pulling, searching and finding. I feel a breeze on my foot as I pull it up. The creature has struck the wall just beneath me.

I pause, listening. The thing is not moving. The impact has either killed it or knocked it unconscious. I'm not sure which, but the smell of blood fills my nose a moment later. I feel my instincts pulling me away from the wall. Finish the kill! Eat the flesh! Sleep! The cycle beckons.

Then I feel the surface beneath my raised hand. The texture is no different than the wall, but it is deep. I reach as far as I can and know my hand has reached the top. I forget the egg-monster and ignore the hamster. Ten seconds later I'm standing on top of the fifteen foot wall that has been my prison.

I am free.

But the glory of escape is short-lived. A solid wall stretches out before me. I follow it around, finding a two foot deep ledge surrounding the pit. For a moment I think I am a prisoner once more. Then I see a spot of black on the far side. A tunnel. I run for it and soon find myself squatting in front of a small hole in the wall about three feet wide and perhaps two tall. But the size is not consistent. This was not a hewn out crawlspace. There are rises in the tiny space, and rocks.

A year before coming to Antarctica I went to Polar Caves in New Hampshire, with Justin and my parents. After the guide told me which hand-holds to take and how to twist my body, I easily maneuvered through the Lemon Squeeze. I imagine getting through this space will be similar. There is only one way through. Getting it wrong will send me back, or worse, leave me stuck.

I turn back to the pit, feeling its pull for me increasing. Then I smell something coming from the tunnel. Food. Cooked food. And I suddenly remember what I've been missing. I enter the tunnel without looking back, and as it turns out, without looking forward. Ten minutes into my own personal Lemon Squeeze and I'm stuck.

18

I will not cry. Wedged tight inside Antarctica's esophagus, I can feel my claustrophobia building. But I will not cry. I am stronger than that now. The last time I felt the world closing in around me was in the back seat of my parents' car on the way to Logan airport. Escaping that predicament was as easy as shifting the luggage. The spot I'm in now presents a far greater challenge.

Without thinking, I pushed myself into a gap that was too small. I ignored the pressure on my chest and pushed onward, desperate for freedom. What I got was stuck. Both arms are wedged forward, pinned in front of me. They are useless for pulling, or pushing. So I won't be going back the way I came. I can now recall clearly what I ignored before. A second branch off to the right, larger than the straight shot I chose.

Like the Orange Crush, I think. Too big or simply not brave enough, my father and mother always took the Orange Crush over the Lemon Squeeze at Polar Caves. It's a slightly more roundabout path, but all that's required to pass through is a simple crouch. This Lemon Squeeze had an Orange Crush alternative, and I failed to take it.

It's a lesson, I think. Slow down. A mistake down here, whether pitted against an egg-monster or squeezing through a crevice, can be deadly. That's when I realize that this must be part of the test too. Whoever took me is seeing if I'll survive. It's a test I'm meant to survive, but that doesn't mean I can't fail. Of course, things could be worse. Somehow I can still see, despite the absence of crystals in the walls here. The air is fresher. And I can hear something ahead. A swish of something—water, wind, something else—I don't know.

But what really keeps me from panicking is the fact that I have a plan. I don't like it, but it should work. The largest part of my body is my ribcage. Despite bulking up on egg-monster meat, my stomach is still slim and according to my mom, Vincent men have skinny butts. So if I can get my ribs through the small space, the rest of me can follow.

But that's going to hurt.

A lot.

My ribs are partially compressed already, wedged in stone. As a result, my breaths are shallow and quick. Getting enough oxygen to stay conscious is an effort. If I hadn't focused on the task I might have passed out already. Time is critical.

Unable to see behind me, I move my feet from side to side,

bending them as close to my body as I can. Once I find purchase, they will provide the force I need to squeeze through. I find a good sized rise on the floor for my right foot and a crack in the wall big enough to slip my toes inside.

I breathe faster, hoping to increase the amount of oxygen in my system. It will soon be starved, but the effort simply taxes my body, so I stop. And rather than suck in a deep breath, I push it out. I force the air from my lungs, shrinking them down and reducing the pressure on my ribs. I know its time to move when I feel my back come away from the tight ceiling.

I push.

I slip forward.

The skin of my bare chest clings to the rough stone, slowing my progress. Each rib compresses as I move through the tiny space, bending near to breaking before popping through. If not for the stone grit gripping my skin, I would already be through.

I push harder.

A different kind of pain flashes into my mind. It's not dull like the constant pressure. It's sharp. And wet. The stone has opened a wound. The sudden pain causes me to suck in a breath.

It's a mistake.

My chest expands quickly. The ribs currently in the stone's grip bend, and then snap. This deeper welling of pain brings a scream from my mouth. Not of anguish, but of anger. I shove hard with my feet while the scream carries the air from my lungs. My body slips forward, the movement lubricated by my blood.

With a final pop of rib over stone, I launch from the stone orifice and land on my side. Despite the pain in my chest from both internal and external wounds, I laugh, which of course increases the pain. But this doesn't bother me, because I'm moving again.

I choose my path more deliberately, backtrack when things get too tight and try multiple handhold arrangements before committing myself. I make remarkable time, slipping through the bowels of the South Pole like some kind of worm.

After rounding a tight corner, I stop when a breeze tickles my face. It's wet and fresh. I ignore my learned caution and rush through the final stretch of tunnel. Then I'm free.

I'm in a cavern, perhaps forty feet across and twice as tall as it is wide. A waterfall pours down from the upper right, pooling in the middle and then disappearing down a hole on the left. A kind of tunnel vision overcomes me and I run for the swirling pool. Had I heeded the lessons learned in the cave—caution, patience, observation—I would have noted the cooling embers of a fire. I would have seen the packs of supplies. The tools. The meat hung to dry. More than that, I would have seen *him*.

Of course, he makes himself impossible to ignore. He allows me to reach the water, to cup it in my hands and raise it to my lips. Then he strikes. His arm goes around my throat and squeezes. The water flies from my hands as I reach up and take hold of his arm. My climbing claws stab into his flesh, creating six neat puncture wounds. But he shows no reaction. He simply squeezes tighter.

He drags me away from the water and tosses me away like I'm a bag of something vile.

The stone floor is unforgiving when I land on my broken ribs.

I roll to ease the pain in my chest, but in doing so lay my back onto the still hot embers. I feel a sharp sting, and the sound of my sizzling skin is quickly drowned out by my scream. I roll off the fire, and still feeling the heat, I make for the water once more.

He strikes again. This time with both fists. He strikes my chest, knocking the air from my lungs and sending me flying over the extinguished fire. My back slaps against the smooth stone wall, pushing a stuck-on ember further in. The pain clouds my mind, but his message gets through—the water is off limits.

I brush the back of my hand over my back, freeing the hot ember and reducing the pain. As I catch my breath, I look at my foe, who has emerged from the shadows.

He is a man, and for that I am grateful. But he is unlike any man I have seen before. He's hunched forward, concealing his height, which I place around six feet. He's skinny. Skinnier than me. But he's strong. His muscles are unbelievably defined and snaked with thick veins. A small piece of cloth covers his waist and groin, but he's otherwise naked, like me. His body is remarkably clean and pale white, nearly translucent. His face and body are hairless, but his head holds thickly clumped, blood-red hair that hangs down to his shoulder. I'd seen the hair before, but up close, the feature that catches my attention is his face. It's covered in wrinkles.

He's an old man, I think.

I look at my climbing claws and think about how easy it was to use them against the egg-monsters. Could an old man be any harder? Something deep within revolts at the idea. He's a human. They were food. Could I really just kill him?

I could, I think.

And he reads my mind.

"You may try once," he says, his English perfect and proper, tinged with a British accent. But the sound is wet and rough. Barely human. He steps to the side, giving me a clear path around the burning embers. This makes no sense.

"You want me to kill you?" I ask.

"If you can kill me, you are already fit to take my place."

Take his place? As what?

I don't bother asking. To my surprise, I charge.

My hands are gripped into fists, the one inch teeth extending from my knuckles. I aim for his throat like I would the belly of an eggy. One slice. That's all it would take. And the man who brought me to this hell-on-earth, the fiend who took me away from my parents and everyone else I care about, would be dead.

My fist cuts through the air, headed for the man's neck. But it finds only empty space. The old man moves like lightning, sidestepping the attack and striking my back. I fall forward, landing half-way in the pool. Without thought, I gulp in a drink. The water is fresh and cold. The distraction nearly costs me my life.

A pounding pressure smashes into my back. The man is on top of me. I push against the pool floor, but find it slippery with algae. He grips my long hair and shoves me down. I shout and thrash, helpless in his hands. My lungs begin to burn. My broken ribs pulse with pain with each heartbeat.

As the urge to breathe becomes unbearable, I resign myself to my fate and stop fighting. My mind turns to the past, to those I've lost, but as the images take root, he pulls me up.

Sounding like a howler monkey, I breathe hard. Despite filling my lungs, each breath seems to have no effect. He drags me over the stone floor by my hair and shoves me into the corner.

I shiver, but not from the cold. Coming so close to death has broken some part of me that had yet to break. As my breathing evens out, I pull my legs to my chest and look at the floor, afraid to meet the eyes of my captor.

His feet approach and stop in front of me. The toe nails are thick and yellow. Possibly sharpened as well. By the way his lower legs bend, I can tell he's squatting in front of me, but I don't look up.

"You will stay in this corner until I tell you otherwise," he said. "Understand?"

I nod.

He strikes my head. The pain is sharp, but doesn't cause injury. "Speak your replies. Head nods do no good in the dark."

"Yes, sir."

"Do not call me, sir," he says, his voice even now.

I'm not sure what to call him, but I suspect the truth. "Master?"

He chuckles. "Were you lucky, that might be true. You will meet your master when you are ready."

"What should I call you, then?"

I see his hand lower. He takes my chin and raises my head. My eyes meet his—dark black saucers surrounded by bloodshot white. He smiles a rotting grin. "You can call me Ninnis."

19

"Sit," Ninnis says. And I obey, settling down against the stone wall. We've been at this for some time. I recognize that he's treating me like a dog, that he's *training* me like a dog. The simple commands of sit, stay and come are the basics of canine obedience. I should be revolted by the idea, but I really don't mind.

I'm fed once a day, sometimes after begging and always his leftovers. I'm not sure what it is I'm eating—it's not egg-monster—but it's cooked. He rations out my water, pouring it in a depression in the floor from which I sip it. My wounds are healing well, though I'll have more than a few messy scars.

I contemplated escape only once. He was asleep, lying by the waterfall. I thought if I were quiet enough I might be able to dive into the river and let it pull me away. One step forward, just one, and I saw his muscles tense. He somehow sensed my movement. Or my thoughts. I'm not sure which.

But I wouldn't do that now. I'm seeing things differently.

My time in the pit with the egg monsters made me strong and toughened me inside and out. My passage through the tunnel made me cautious and thoughtful. He is helping me. Preparing me. He spoke of my master, who I believe is also his master. He is acting under compulsion, but he's also working hard to make sure I survive.

So I appreciate Ninnis. I listen to him. Without him I would be lost.

I sit in my spot while Ninnis prepares and cooks a limb of some creature. I'm not sure where it came from. I suspect he hunts while I sleep. The meat has a pungent odor, but my mouth waters nonetheless. I whine.

"Wait," he says.

He turns the meat once, letting both sides cook. I watch the fat drip away and sizzle in the small fire fueled by the defecation of creatures I have yet to see. "Tell me about your father," Ninnis asks.

This is the first time he has spoken to me aside from commands. I'm so taken aback that I fail to answer.

"Speak!" he shouts over his shoulder. Not answering now would result in a beating. I've endured four already, for various offenses. But they were necessary. I'm sure the lessons will save me some day.

I search for something to say about my father, but can't think of anything. I try to imagine him so that I might describe his face. But all I see is a blur, as though the lens peering into my perfect memory has been smudged. I try to imagine my mother. The results are the same.

Ninnis is on his feet now, storming toward me. I tense for a beating, but he stops. In one hand he holds the roast meat, its juices dripping down over his hand and forearm. In the other hand, he holds a knife. I've seen the blade before. It's very old. About five inches long and sporting an engraved wooden handle. I've only seen bits of the engraving, but I think it's some kind of military insignia.

"Speak, boy!" Ninnis screams at me. "Can't you remember your own father?"

"I—I can't," I say. "I'm trying to remember him, anything about him, but I can't."

Ninnis steps back, all hints of anger erased. "And your mother?"

"Nothing."

"Stand," he says.

I obey, casting my eyes to his feet like a subservient animal. He takes my hand and places his knife in it. When he lifts my hand, my eyes follow. The tip of the knife is placed over Ninnis's heart. He lets go of my hand, leaving the blade in my control. "I want you to kill me," he says.

I stare at the knife, which has already nicked his skin.

"Kill me," he repeats.

It would be so easy. A quick thrust and I would be free. But like a lost dog, I would simply roam the underworld, unsure, hungry and longing for the one who keeps me safe and fed. I can't kill Ninnis any more than I can kill myself.

"Ninnis, no!" I shout, dropping the knife and wrapping my arms around him.

He stands there with his arms out for a moment, then returns my embrace. I can't see his face, but I know he's smiling. After stepping back from me, Ninnis holds out the roast limb. "Your reward," he says. "Come. Eat with me."

A true smile creeps onto my face and I sit with him by the fire. The meat is tender and fatty. I eat with gusto, but do not fill my stomach. When I place the meat down and wrap it in skins as I've watched Ninnis do, he nods in approval. I have learned far more than obedience during my time here. Ninnis has modeled moderation and survival skills I will need. I know which stones will light a fire. I know which skins are best for water and which are best for meat. I know to keep clean and free of infection.

We live like subterranean Neanderthals for a time, getting to know each other—two men living off the land—like hunters. I enjoy this time of bonding, of camaraderie. Ninnis is as good a friend as I've ever had.

I sleep and dream of egg-monsters. They dance around me. They fall at my feet, worshiping me, chanting the name, "Nephil."

The vision fades as I'm nudged awake. Ninnis stands above me, his belongings slung over his back in a bundle of skin. "Time to go," he says. "There's something I want to show you."

I gather my things, bundling food, scooping water in a skin and donning my climbing claws (Ninnis was impressed by them, but only recently told me so). He leads me through a tight passage. It's tall enough to stand in, but very narrow. On the other side, Ninnis says, "Keep track of the small spaces you see. Remember them and they will save your life."

I nod, but am not sure what could threaten Ninnis's life. He seems a King in this underground realm. The tunnel beyond the tight fissure is vast, carved out by the river that falls into what was our living space. Erosion has smoothed out the river bed, but a sea of boulders skirts the eight foot wide waterway. It's over these giant stones that we travel. Crystals glitter from the cavern ceiling and from many of the boulders. Ninnis stays in the darkest parts of the tunnel. He's following a path I think he has traveled many times in the past.

After several hours I realize that we have been heading steadily up, but it's not until the first hint of daylight strikes me that I realize how far up we're going. The distant light is really just a speck, but feels intense on my eyes.

"Here," he says, holding something out to me. I take the strange thing and look at it for a moment. Then I remember what they are and what they're for.

"Sunglasses," I say.

"Got them from a gatherer."

I stop. He hasn't mentioned gatherers before. In fact, he has said very little of the world in which I now live. "A gatherer?"

"Later," he says. "Put them on when the light becomes unbearable, but you will eventually have to operate in daylight without them."

"We go outside?"

He nods. "Occasionally. If ordered."

"Like when you got me?" I ask.

"Exactly."

I follow him over a line of stones that looks like a ruined wall. "What are we called?"

He looks back at me, confused by the question. I explain. "If there are gatherers, then there must be names for everything else in this world."

A smile stretches across his face. "You're quick. I can see why they chose you, Ull."

Ninnis has been calling me by my middle name all along. So much so that I'm not sure what my first or last name was. I know I had them, but like everything else down here, my memory of them is a fog. All that remains is Ull. And when Ninnis finally answers my question, I know why he chose to use that name.

"There are gatherers, warriors, seekers, feeders, breeders, thinkers, and us."

I lean forward expectantly.

"The hunters."

I smile wide. Ull, the Norse god of the hunt. This pleases me.

One hundred yards from the tunnel exit, I can no longer bear the light. I put on the sunglasses and find they only offer partial relief. Ninnis is squinting but requires no artificial aid. The exit is a small hole dug into a wall of blue ice. Through the tunnel is a circle of blue sky. The tunnel is horizontal, so I realize we must be high up. Inside a mountain perhaps.

Ninnis pauses by the exit and reaches into his pack. He pulls out a small device and holds it out to me. I take it and flip the copper cylinder in my hands. For a moment, I don't recognize it. Then, in a flash, I do. I take hold of one end and pull. The telescope expands.

I think I've used one before. Maybe even had one of my own.

"You like it?" Ninnis asks.

"Very much."

"Good."

"It's for me?"

Ninnis nods. "A gift."

"For what?"

Ninnis chuckles like I'm silly for asking. "For your birthday, of course."

Some part of my brain, perhaps the part in charge of numbers, isn't totally blurred out and I think, *I've been here for eleven months.*

"How is that possible?" I ask.

He understands what I'm asking. To me, and possibly him, it feels like a month, two at the most, has passed.

"Time is different here," he says. "Outside, time moves faster. For us, we only met weeks ago. In that time outside, several months have passed. If I were to tell you how long I have lived here, I might say ten years. But in the outside world, perhaps one hundred years have passed.

"You're one hundred years old?" I ask, eyes wide.

Ninnis grins. "I was thirty-four when I arrived."

"One hundred and thirty-four years old...How is that possible?"

"A gift that now belongs to you. Your body will age as though it were still in the outside world despite your perception of time being different. But your body will resist the deterioration of age with uncommon resilience."

"And when I reach your age, I will train my replacement?"

Ninnis shakes his head. "From what I understand, you are to be the last hunter."

"The last?"

"Destined for some greater purpose. You need not worry yourself with such things right now." Ninnis takes my shoulder in his
hand. He motions toward the tunnel. "Let's go try out that spyglass, eh?"

20

It takes five minutes for my eyes to adjust to the light enough to see, even with the sunglasses on. Of course, it doesn't help that the sky is nearly cloudless and most of Antarctica is covered in a sheet of sun-reflective white. I'd like nothing more than to retreat into my subterranean home, but Ninnis insists that I try out my birthday present.

The fact that it's my birthday hardly seems deserving of mention or gift. It's a tradition of the outside world, and I doubt I ever considered it a day of any significance. But I cannot deny the gift from Ninnis. Rejecting it would be an insult to the man who has given me so much already.

So I follow him over the snow-covered mountain. My bare feet sink into the white powder, disappearing beneath a foot of the stuff. It slows our progress, but we make it to our destination—a bare ledge—in good time.

Ninnis lies down on the gray stone, which is magically free of snow, and I take the spot next to him. Below us, the mountain stretches down, a long slope of white ending in a mixture of stone and snow. And this leads to a mixture of bright colors. Reds. Blues. Yellows. The colors make me sneer. They're revolting. Like a blemish on the pure landscape. Beyond them is a long stretch of white that ends in a sliver of blue ocean.

Ninnis points toward the sea of bright colors. "What do you think?" He motions to the telescope. "Give it a try."

I pop open the telescope and place it to my eye. The bright colors pop out as large metal boxes. Even uglier up close. Between the boxes are people, bundled in thick clothing. I observe them for several minutes, watching the lazy way they walk, the grime covering their hands and the gray snow beneath their feet. "Disgusting," I say.

"Quite," Ninnis agrees. "How do you feel?"

"Angry."

"Why?"

I put no thought into the answer, speaking quickly and honestly. "I hate them."

"Good," Ninnis says. "Very good."

A strong wind rolls down the mountain behind and over us. It scrapes away the top layer of snow and pelts our backs. The fast moving flakes sting my skin, but I've learned to deal with pain far greater than this.

Ninnis taps my arm. "I'm impressed."

I turn to him. "With what?"

"Your resistance to the cold."

I look at my skin. It's pale white and like Ninnis's, partially translucent. I can see the blue of my veins below. I turn my attention to Ninnis. His skin looks similar, but is pocked with goose bumps. He feels the cold. I decide to keep the fact that I feel nothing to myself. I don't want Ninnis to think I'm strange. I don't know why I fear that, but I do. He might stop being my friend.

"There," he says, pointing beyond the blocks of color. "Quickly."

I look through the spyglass and focus beyond the ugly city. A large airplane is parked on the ice. An airport, I think. The word sounds foreign in my mind, but I know what it means. A treaded vehicle pulls up to the staircase hanging down from the side of the plane. A line of people file out of the vehicle and rush up the stairs into the airplane. *Weaklings.*

The stream of people is followed by a final pair. They're moving slower than the others, not worrying about the cold. Halfway to the staircase one of them stops. It's a woman. I can tell by her shape. *Brick house*, I think, but I'm not entirely certain what it means so I keep it to myself.

The woman falls to her knees and is caught by the man. He holds her for a moment, while her body shakes. *Crybaby.* Then the man has her up and moving again.

"What do you think of them?" Ninnis asks, peering through a set of binoculars I did not see him take out.

"The man and woman?"

"Yes."

I watch as the woman turns her face to the mountains as though looking for something. Her face is twisted, like she's in pain, and for a moment I think she is looking right at me. Her gaze makes me uncomfortable, so I look at the man instead. He just looks sad, but unlike the woman seems resigned to whatever tragedy is making the woman weep. "Crybaby," I say as a second wind rolls down the mountainside.

"Indeed," he says. "Anything else?"

"I hope they all leave. This isn't their home."

"Very intuitive."

"Who are they?" I ask.

"They came here to look for something."

"Did they find it?"

"No."

"Will they ever?" I'm not sure why I care whether they do or not, but I can't help wondering.

"Never," Ninnis replies with conviction. "It is lost to them forever."

I watch them take the steps slowly and enter the plane. When they're finally out of sight I feel restless. The need to get back underground overwhelms me. When I turn to Ninnis to ask about leaving, I find his head turned toward the sky.

I follow his eyes up and find the blue sky above us blotted out by a roiling storm cloud. "Where did that come from?" I ask.

"I was wondering the same thing." He looks at me and is about to speak again, but a rumble we can both feel distracts him. He looks up. His eyes widen. Then he has my arm clutched in his hand. "Run, boy, run!"

I glance up as we backtrack toward the cave entrance. A wall of white is rolling down the mountainside. *Avalanche*, I think.

Faster than I thought possible, we're back at the cave entrance. Ninnis motions me through. "Go!"

I dive in, sliding through the slippery tunnel with ease. Before I'm through I feel a wave of pressure pushing behind me. When I reach the cave and turn around to pull Ninnis through, I find him missing. The tunnel is sealed with packed snow. I dive into the tunnel and crawl to its end. I pummel and scrape the fresh cork of snow. But it is packed tight. Not even the sharp tips of my climbing claws can break through.

Ninnis is gone.

My friend is gone.

I mourn his loss for only a moment—sadness results in death—Ninnis taught me that, and then I turn to the tunnel leading back down into the heart of the mountain, and beyond that perhaps, the heart of Antarctica itself. I take a tentative step forward, the first tingle of fear taking root. I have no idea what waits for me in the dark, nor how to reach my unknown master. I am lost without my guide but—no.

I am not afraid.

I have survived worse.

Ninnis told me I was a hunter. Like him.

I glance down at my claws. I feel the weight of my pack and the supplies it contains. I am ready.

It's time to hunt.

21

There are twenty-one small fissures in the walls of the underground river tunnel. These are the nooks and crannies I think I can fit through, but just barely. Fifteen more are tunnels I can crawl through easily, though I don't know whether or not they shrink or expand later on. I suppose that's true with all of them. Each could taper off to nothing.

Have patience, I tell myself. *Explore each tunnel. Become as familiar with this place as Ninnis.*

Three tunnels are tall enough for me to walk through, perhaps eight feet tall. Only one really counts as a branching cavern. It's a stone's throw away from the bottom of the river tunnel, where Ninnis and I first entered from our waterfall hideaway. It's close to thirty feet tall. What's strangest about it is that it seems to be the most worn tunnel. Many stones are crushed flat. The floor in the center is worn smooth, as though well-traveled. This seems like the most likely avenue to reach the ones Ninnis spoke of. Also the most likely place to find something to hunt.

Walking alone in the sparse dark space of the new cavern, I find myself relaxing, feeling right at home. I have a sense of having been here before. An uncommon familiarity. But I know I've never been here before. While I can't see my past clearly anymore, I sense it wasn't here. Or was it? Some parts of my memory—very old images—remain less fogged. I suspect because they are memories of Antarctica, perhaps of some significant event.

I focus on recalling this memory. Something about it feels important. Before I can recall anything with clarity, I hear a sound. It's a gentle scraping, amplified by the echoing tunnel.

Crouching low, I advance. Boulders on the side of the tunnel conceal my approach. I move in silence like Ninnis taught me, keeping three limbs in contact with the stone at all times. Stealth and balance are keys to a successful hunt.

A scent tickles my nose. I suck it in slowly, tasting it. I cannot recognize the specific origin of the odor, but I know it's blood. A fresh kill. I move closer. The scraping is just on the other side of a tall, obelisk-like stone. I chance a look.

My head pokes into view for the briefest of moments. But in that time I'm able to take everything in. The fresh kill is a large albino centipede, perhaps the size of my arm. Ninnis cooked one once. I have come to enjoy a lot of questionable meals, but the centipede was one of the more revolting. Even Ninnis cringed at its flavor.

The creature atop the death-coiled centipede must lack taste buds entirely, because its head is buried beneath the white exoskeleton shaking back and forth feverishly, devouring the slick insides with abandon. As for the predator, I'm not sure what it is. It's hunched over, so I can only guess its true height, but it appears to be five feet long with two feet of tail and another two of neck. Its torso is about the size of a cocker spaniel. Its hind legs smack of ostrich, but the claws on its three toes are infinitely sharper. Its forelimbs are short, but dexterous, tipped with tiny hands that grip the centipede carcass. Shiny green skin, perhaps scaled, covers most of the body except for the back, where it is patterned with splotches of maroon. Though I fight the conclusion—it's beyond imagining—I can't help thinking that this is a small dinosaur.

How can I see all this? I wonder. I know there is no light here, but I can make out details like this without problem. *I'll have to ask Ninnis.* But Ninnis is dead. A question for another time, then.

Right now, it's time to hunt.

The creature doesn't see, hear or smell me coming. With its head buried inside the centipede's gullet, its fate is sealed. Perhaps if the ground was less firm, a vibration from one of my footfalls might give me away. But the cave floor is solid rock.

I approach it from behind, arms tense. My plan is simple and according to Ninnis, the safest way to make a kill. Attack from behind, slice the neck and then retreat while the prey bleeds out. "Many denizens of the underground are equipped with sharp claws and teeth," Ninnis told me. "And most thrash wildly about as their life comes to a close. Best to distance yourself until the life goes out of them."

One quick, deep cut and then retreat. The whole attack should take seconds.

But I never get that far.

I hear breathing.

Not mine. Not my prey's. It's deep, like the lungs of a large horse.

You fool, I say to myself. Following Ninnis's advice on hunting is no good unless I also follow his rules on survival. I paid attention to my prey, but not the world around us. I took its size for granted, assuming it was full grown and never once considering it might be the young of something larger.

Less than a day since Ninnis departed this world and I'm about to join him. He had so much faith in me. I shake my head, determined not to let him down.

I turn to face the new threat while the baby finishes its meal, oblivious to what is going on behind it.

A face stares at me from the shadows, hanging low over a boulder. I can't see its body, but I sense it is tense, coiled and ready to pounce. The face is colored green, like the baby's and sports a ruddy splotch shaped like an arrow on its snout, which tapers up from two large nostrils and ends with a large crest behind the eyes. And those eyes hold my attention. Two yellow orbs with black serpentine slits stare back at me.

I hold my breath when the head slides forward, emerging from the shadows. A long neck follows, then two short arms. I call them short, despite each being longer than my arms, but in com-

parison to its body, which is massive, the arms are disproportio-
nate. I see two crouched hind legs in the darkness and hear its tail
swishing back and forth like an agitated cat's.

Aim for the eyes, I think as it stops only a few feet from my
face. It sniffs, taking in my scent with deep breaths. It leans closer, nudging my shoulder as it smells...my hair?

The thing, which is without doubt a living dinosaur, snaps its
head back like it's been slapped in the face. The dinosaur turns its
head up and opens its mouth, revealing two rows of needle-sharp
teeth, and calls out two quick barks.

Two distant barks reply.

Then four more even further away.

There are more of these things! Many more!

As it brings its head back down, I have no doubt the dinosaur
will pounce, so I make the first move. I swing out with an open
palm thinking *wax on*, but not recalling the reference. The tips of
my climbing claws dig into the beast's forehead, cutting the flesh
until striking the thick bone of its eyebrow and glancing away.

It's a paltry distraction, but it's enough.

With a roar, it lifts its head for a moment.

When it lowers again, I am off and running.

Like the young dinosaur, I can't hear anything as my rushing
blood courses past my ears. I suspect it runs as silently as I do,
too, because despite the thing's size (I'd guess twenty feet from
snout to the tip of its tail) I still can't feel any vibrations beneath
my feet. I'm breathing too hard to smell anything. And like my
mother says, I don't have eyes in the back of my head.

My mother?

The distraction nearly costs me my life.

The river saves it.

I hit the water and fall down as the dinosaur's jaws snap shut above me. The water sweeps me away. As the water pushes me downstream and pummels me into stones, I get a look back. The dinosaur has not given up the chase. It pounds through the water behind me.

I see three small tunnels rush by. Each would have provided refuge from the ancient predator. The tunnel ends up ahead and I see the crevice that leads to the waterfall hideaway. I swim for shore, but the current is too strong, and the river bottom is too polished to get my footing.

I pass my salvation in a blur before being sucked underwater. The river tunnel ends in a whirlpool before descending deeper. I'm pulled into it, spinning madly. I can't see. I can't breathe. And the pain of my head striking something hard registers for only a moment. As consciousness fades, I think, did I remember my mother? The question is answered by darkness.

22

I regain consciousness underwater. My lungs burn. My head throbs. And all around me, the water rushes. But I don't panic. I have come closer to drowning and do not fear it. Again, thanks to Ninnis.

Just as I decide to swim with the current, turning my body forward, the river falls out from under me. As I flip, head over heels, I see snapshots of the river, now an endless waterfall, turning into a broad, fine mist next to me. I see water far below, frothing with white where the waterfall meets it. This water stretches out and away further than I can see, but there is a shoreline to the left and something else. Something large.

I focus on the approaching water. I vaguely remember hearing about someone jumping off a bridge into water to kill himself. I'll reach terminal velocity—one hundred twenty miles per hour—in about fifteen seconds. At that speed the water will feel like solid stone. I've been falling for six seconds.

Ten seconds into the fall, there is no more time to calculate. I strike the water, feet first (this saves my life) and plunge deep under water. The impact doesn't kill me or break any bones, but it does fog my mind nearly to the point of unconsciousness. I must have forgotten to breathe while falling because my lungs scream for air. I know the surface must be near, but in the weightless dark I don't know which way is up and with my lungs empty, I lack the buoyancy to float.

I'll float just fine once my dead body fills with gas, I think.

I swim. I have no choice. But I choose the wrong direction. When my head strikes the hard bottom, I know this for sure. Spots dance in my vision, possibly from lack of oxygen, possibly from the impact. Either way, I'm disoriented.

My body fails me, going limp. My mouth is close to opening. My vision fades. I slide to the bottom, which now feels like a soft cushion and use the last of my energy to clutch my mouth shut. I feel water rushing over me, pulling my hair over my face. And then, once again, darkness claims me.

* * *

I open my eyes and see a rock cut so perfectly at a ninety degree angle that I know it's manmade. This thought keeps me from closing my eyes again, despite how badly I want to. I'm battered from head to toe. My lungs hurt. Muscles I didn't know I had cry out in pain. But the carved stone is a mystery my mind cannot ignore.

After squeezing my eyes shut a few times, I can focus beyond what lies right in front of me. I twist my head, turning it down an incline of several more angled cuts. A massive staircase. Each step is four feet deep and just as tall. The stone steps descend into what I can only describe as a lake. It reaches out to the dark horizon which sweeps up and over me, concealing the cavern ceiling that must be a half mile high. Maybe more.

I roll over, sit up and freeze. A pair of black eyes stares at me from the water. Unlike most of the monsters living underground, I recognize this one. It's a Weddell seal with an unmistakable patchwork of dark brown and beige skin. Exactly how I can identify this creature, I can't recall, but the only thing that makes me doubt its identity is that we're far underground.

"How did you get here?" I ask it.

It responds by sliding back into the dark water.

Something about seeing it move triggers a faded memory. Not from my past. This one is recent. The soft bottom of the lake, where I should have drowned. The water rushing past. This out-of-place seal saved my life.

"Don't go," I say. As it slips away, I stand and hop down the steps and into the water. But it's gone before I can reach it. It surfaces again, thirty feet out, rolling on the surface to catch a breath before diving back down. A smile creeps onto my face as eight more humps rise and fall. A family. It's nice to know not everything in this subterranean world wants to eat me.

Before turning away, I see my dim reflection in the water. I haven't seen my face in so long, I feel like I'm looking at a stranger. My skin is paper white. The blue around my pupils, which are open wide, has been reduced to a thin line of color. And my hair is streaked dark red. There appears to be as much blond hair as red, but...hasn't it always been that way?

I tire of looking at my face and haul myself out of the water and onto the lowest step. I then set myself to the task of climbing the steep staircase. Eight steps in all. Thirty-two vertical feet. At the top, I need to stop and catch my breath. I bend over, hands on knees, in through the nose, out through the mouth. Did Ninnis teach me that?

When I stand upright I'm looking at something I would have never thought possible. The staircase is just the beginning of something huge. Something ancient. It can best be described as a temple complex. There are several small step pyramids surrounding a larger, spiraling tower, like a Sumerian ziggurat. Its top is concealed by darkness. Obelisks and statues line the streets, though many are broken. In fact, the place looks like it has been through a war. A few wars, really. The buildings are scarred with gouges and impact craters. A wall that once surrounded much of the site is now a crumbled pile of stones.

As I approach the ancient metropolis I am dwarfed by its scale. Like the four-foot steps, this place was made for, or by, giants. The only standing city gate must be sixty feet tall. The ruined walls, which looked small from a distance are still piled twenty feet high. How tall were they when they still stood? I now know how a mouse feels when it looks at a house. I could disappear inside this place. Hide like a rodent in the nooks and crannies.

I enter the temple court, walking through the massive gates feeling smaller than ever. And more exposed. I pause to get my bearings. I hold my breath and listen. A faint breeze is rolling over the temple from the lake. The air smells clean, like it does after a rainstorm. I see no hints of movement. *I am alone*, I think, which is good. Without my pack and climbing claws I am defenseless. In fact, I'd better find a weapon of some kind in this place. I will soon need to make a kill and eat.

As I round a black obelisk covered in circular symbols that look vaguely familiar, I come upon the most massive statue I can recall seeing. *It's like the Colossus of Rhodes*, I think. But this giant isn't standing guard over a harbor, or even looking out at the water. He sits atop a fallen obelisk, back rigid, head looking straight. I cannot see the face, only its back.

As I walk slowly closer, details resolve and something starts nagging at my subconscious. The statue has been painted in dull colors. Brown armor. Gray skin. Red hair covered by a Viking-esque helmet covered in what appear to be rows of upturned teeth that remind me of the dinosaur's open jaws.

Red hair.

When my subconscious finally breaks through, it's screaming.

Who builds a statue on a *fallen* obelisk!

I stop.

This is no statue.

The red hair is not painted.

This giant...is alive.

I take a nervous step back. My footing is firm. My step silent. I pause before stepping again, sensing a shift in the breeze. It's now at my back. At *his* back, too. The movement is so subtle I almost miss it. The giant's head cocked to the side.

For a moment I think my presence has gone unnoticed, but then see a twitch in the mammoth man's calf muscle. He is shifting his weight to stand. Once on his feet, the giant would stand nearly twenty-five feet tall and could cover the distance between us in four strides.

Though I feel a tinge of shame for running once again, I see no alternative, and put my feet to the stone. Silence pursues me, but I suspect the thing is simply playing with me, giving me a head start. A moment later, my suspicion proves correct as the first thundering footfall gives chase.

I don't look back as I pass back beneath the gate. My eyes are on what's in front of me. A small section of cave wall to my right is essentially a dead end. To my left are the four foot steps. Even if I manage to make it to the steps and vault down them without twisting an ankle, what would I do then? Swim like the world's slowest minnow. The giant would pluck me from the water.

I head for the wall, hoping for a crack in its surface. The ground beneath me shakes. Unlike the large dinosaur, this giant is heavy and far from light-footed. As he gets closer, the vibrations nearly knock me forward.

As I near the wall, its details leap out. I see two large cracks, but both are five feet from the cave floor. Getting inside would take time. And I don't have any time to spare. In fact, I think the giant is right behind me.

Then why hasn't he squashed me or picked me up? I wonder.

Not caring about the answer, I focus on the wall again and find my escape route. At the bottom of the wall is a horizontal crevice about a foot high and six feet wide. I can fit. And quickly.

A few feet from the wall, I dive forward and slide across the gritting stone floor. I ignore the pain as several wounds tear open on my chest and hands and pull myself into the wall. Just as my feet slide in behind me, a thunderous boom shakes the tunnel. I glance back to see the giant's large, six-toed bare foot just behind me.

Was he trying to crush me? Or taunt me?

I pull myself deeper, caring more about escape than answers, but get my answer when the giant begins laughing. His voice is deep and rumbles through me. I can feel the pulsing laugh in my chest. It chases me into the darkness, stripping away my confidence and filling me with a fear that goes far beyond physical pain or death.

That thing...that man...was evil.

And I hope I'll never see him again.

23

"You're dead now," I say to the small, arm-sized centipede. The thing had put up quite a fight, thrashing and trying to bite, but the rock in my hand proved too much for it in the end. I know now why the small dinosaur picked it for a meal—centipedes are stupid. It didn't take too much effort to sneak up on the thing. If not for its hard shell, my first strike would have killed it. But its carapace was like a turtle shell and breaking through took four solid whacks.

Now the thing is leaking its white, cream cheese-like innards all over a boulder. The sight and smell of the thing makes me pause, but I haven't eaten in days. I scoop some of the fleshy sludge up with my fingers. For a moment I wonder if it is poisonous.

No, I think, *the dinosaur ate it.*

Holding my breath, I put my hand in my mouth and scrape the stuff off with my teeth. I swallow quickly and repeat the process. The centipede tastes as bad as I thought it would, but it's settling nicely in my stomach. When I'm done I rinse the taste out of my mouth at a small spring I found. The caves are covered in small springs and finding water is rarely a problem anymore. Food is a different problem, because food here either runs away or tries to eat me.

But I won't need to eat again for at least another day, so I take some time to explore. Keeping track of where I've been is simple. My perfect memory, at least back to when I first came here, has assembled a three dimensional map of every place I've been. Today I'm determined to fill in a gap. Then I'll have a three cubic mile territory memorized.

What bothers me about this gap is that I'm not sure what's there. I haven't seen the dinosaurs again, so maybe they nest there. The giant, too. Anything could be there. I tell myself I'm likely to find nothing. There are many large and small tunnels leading out of my territory and creatures as big as those would need territories vastly larger. But still, I'm nervous about what I'll find.

I squeeze through a tight space and for a moment think I've got myself stuck again, but then I'm through and sporting a new scrape on my chest. I ignore the sting and dripping blood as I arrive in a wider, inclined tunnel. It's tall enough to stand in, maybe eight feet tall and four wide. My mind fills in the holes in my mental map. If the tunnel carries on in either direction as straight as it appears to, then one side would reach the large river tunnel and the other would reach the surface.

But I can't just assume this. I need to make sure. So I take the tunnel left, looking for branches along the way. I find none, but thirty minutes later I reach the river. After a quick drink, I backtrack up the tunnel. An hour later, I reach the surface. The entrance to the tunnel is blocked from view by a stone jutting out from the mountain. I step out of the tunnel and find the outside as dark as the inside. It's night. And it's snowing. I crouch in the snow half way up the mountain. It's peaceful out here. I sense that nothing will try to eat me here, and the snow—I eat some—tickles my tongue as it melts. I listen to the tick, tick of snowflakes landing and wonder where I've heard the sound before. I have no memory of it, but ticking doesn't strike me as something new, just something I enjoy.

My stomach isn't rumbling yet, but I know it will be soon. So I head back into the tunnel, destination: river. I hope to find something more significant to eat than a centipede, but I also have no weapon, so something that couldn't make a meal of me would also be spectacular.

As I walk down the tunnel, taking note of the tiny fragments of glimmering stone that help me see, I try to create stone weapons in my mind. How would cave men do it? I'll need a stick. Some rope. And a sharp stone. *A stick on its own might do the job,* I think. *Well, not against a—*

A white square—its whiteness and perfect edges completely foreign in the underground—catches my attention. It's in the middle of the tunnel floor.

How did I not see this before? I wonder.

I don't know, but here it is.

I crouch down to the flat thing. What is it?

Before picking it up, I smell it. There are traces of something I can't place, but have smelled before. I taste it. The same. I place my finger against it and yank it away.

I laugh at my ridiculousness. I'm acting like an ape who discovered fire. I know this is from the outside world, and I know in my core that it is harmless, but something about it has me on edge. As I reach for it I think I would rather be facing down a dinosaur. My cowardice before a piece of paper makes me angry. I snatch it up and turn it around.

It's an image. Two faces have been captured. *A photograph*, I think. *A Polaroid*. I can remember facts about the process of taking photos, of film and development, but nothing beyond that. No real memories. Just information. And the two people in the image are strangers to me.

There is a girl. Dark skin. Light hair. Her head is leaning on a boy's shoulder, his hair as light as hers, though much straighter. And his skin is as white as hers is brown. Both are smiling. Happy. But the bared teeth make me feel like the pair want to eat me. Like they want to tear me apart.

I don't like this image.

I turn it back over, unable to look at it again. I want to destroy it, but find myself unable to do so. *I can fling it outside*, I think. *Let the wind take it away.* I step toward the cave exit again and stop. It feels wrong for some reason. Despite my loathing of the image, my gut says it could be important later on.

So I save it.

Not on my person. That would be unbearable.

I find a thin crack and insert the picture. When it's almost all the way in, I tap it with my finger and it disappears into the space. I peer in after it. I'll need a stick or something thin to pry it out later on.

I stand back. No one will ever know it's there. For a moment I wonder if I'll remember where it is, but make a mental note on my map. If I need this image again, I'll know where it is.

Until then I make a silent vow to avoid this tunnel and the photo that scares me more than being eaten alive.

24

I've adopted a new system of time. Who's to say whether or not it coincides with the twenty-four hour days on the surface? I doubt it, but I have noticed I have regular periods of sleep followed by regular periods of being awake. I suppose I could count out the minutes and translate this into hours, but trying to force time underground to make sense in terms of the above-ground world will only distract me. So I judge days by my waking and sleeping now. But how long is a day really? For all I know it could be a week. It doesn't matter anymore.

According to my new calendar, I've been on my own for a month. It's been twenty days since I found and hid the photo. And in that time I have hunted and been hunted. I have killed and nearly been killed. But, as Ninnis taught me, I have survived.

I have a new weapon. At its core is a staff of very flexible wood.

It's old, and I'm not sure how it got down here, but it bends like a fishing pole, so it follows me through the tightest squeezes, but it's rigid enough to make a good thrusting spear. At one end—the spear end—I have attached a sharpened bone from a dinosaur skeleton. I had hoped to use one of its teeth, but the skull was missing. On the other end—the mace end—is a baseball-sized stone. It's not intimidating to look at, but it's solid, and dense. I fashioned the weapon after realizing there are two types of creatures in the underground. Those that you need to stab. And those that you need to bludgeon.

In addition to the weapon, which I have dubbed *Whipsnap*, I now have a thirty-foot rope created from the skins of several different prey creatures. After skinning the creatures, I dried the skins and then cut them into thin strips, which I then braided together. The line can stretch and hold my weight, even after a deadfall. I learned this the hard way, but now I know.

I have stones for making fire. A collection of dried dung for fueling said fires. And a collection of sharpened bones I use to pry apart, fillet, skewer and otherwise dismantle my meals. I'm a regular subterranean butcher and chef rolled into one.

But I have yet to take down anything bigger than me.

That changes today.

Today is the day I overcome one of my lingering fears. Granted, it's not the biggest specimen I've seen, but it's a start.

My map of the underworld has expanded from three cubic miles to four miles deep and twelve square miles around. The territory is vast and overlaps in several places with the domain of the dinosaurs that I now call Crestosaurs. Cresty for short. Not very Latin sounding, I know, but it's descriptive. The crest atop their heads ranges in size and color on the males. The most dominant have tall, bright red crests. The females have average-sized green colored crests. But the females are also much larger—up to thirty feet long—though they never stand fully upright. Even the biggest stands only fifteen feet high. They are lean, fast and move in packs.

But they hunt alone.

Like this one.

At ten feet long, it's no lightweight, but it's still an adolescent and not the best hunter. It chases after everything it sees, running madly, striking fast. It catches a centipede, toys with it for a moment, then gets distracted by something else further down the tunnel.

We're in a river tunnel I call the Deep River. It's actually very shallow, but it runs about a mile beneath the High River, which drains into the old temple ruins (which I have yet to return to—that is a fear to conquer on another day). This river is wide, nearly forty feet, but the ceiling and floor are covered with stalactites and stalagmites, some of which merge and form columns running floor to ceiling. A scattering of smaller stalagmites makes moving quickly difficult because I'm likely to impale my foot if I'm not careful, but the large ones provide ample hiding places. And this allows me to stalk my prey without fear of detection.

As the young cresty claws at a stone, trying to flip and chase down the small crab-like thing that scuttled beneath it, I sneak up behind. With my free hand and feet, I cling to the larger stalagmites and shift from one to the next, careful to keep my feet out of the rushing water. I've learned not to underestimate any creature in the underworld and I'm not about to start with one that could remove my head in one bite. A drip or splash might be enough to alert the beast to my presence.

I'm within striking range now, just ten feet away. I consider my approach. Silent? Check. Down wind? Check. Out of sight? Check.

Something tickles my foot.

I look down. A long green tendril slides back and forth over my foot. The rest of it disappears into the water. Is it a snake or some kind of worm?

I can't tell, but I've never seen it before, and if it lives down here, it's a predator. I expect the thing to bite into my foot with whatever small jaws it has, but it suddenly disappears beneath the water, as though pulled away.

Pulled away.

The cresty has stopped scraping the rock. I can still smell it, but it's not moving. It's waiting.

For me.

I take a deep breath. It's time.

With a howl I jump out from my hiding spot, Whipsnap held high.

The dinosaur has misjudged my position and nearly falls over with surprise. It may have detected me, but the element of surprise is still on my side. I press the attack, lunging with the spear tip. But the cresty is fast and leaps away.

And now it's angry.

The cresty snaps at me twice, eyeing my weapon. It's smart enough to know rushing into a blade would hurt. But how smart can it be, really? Dinosaurs have what? Almond sized brains?

I lower the spear tip slowly until its point fully pierces the water.

"Out of sight, out of mind," I say. Either emboldened by the disappearance of the spear tip or spurred by my voice, the cresty charges.

Whipsnap earned its name because of its ability to snap back into place. When I lift with my arms, the blade pops back out of the water and rises to meet the dinosaur's chest. The cresty tries to backpedal, but a sudden and fortunate gush of water helps carry it forward. The blade sinks in, but stops at the beast's breastbone.

Had that been the extent of my attack, the cresty might recover, but I am far from done. I have imagined this technique again and again and have practiced on boulders. I know it can work and I put it to the test.

With the blade firmly planted in the cresty's chest, I bend the back end up and over. I can feel the shaft tensing as it bends to the point where I feel it will break, and then beyond. But it doesn't break.

The mace end clocks the dinosaur on the head, stunning it for a moment. But the impact also frees the blade from the breast bone. As I sidestep, the spear end of Whipsnap springs down and out, returning to its straight form. But it has done far more than straighten. When the blade snapped down it was still buried in two inches of flesh. The cresty has been eviscerated.

As its guts fall out, I jump back and wait. The cresty thrashes, slicing its innards to bits. A few minutes later, the thing is dead.

I smile. I have overcome my fear and I'll have food for another month. And by then I might be strong and fast enough to take down one of the grownups.

Before I can really savor my conquest, my smile fades.

Had I still been fighting the cresty, I might have missed it.

A drip.

I'm being hunted.

25

The hunter is good. I haven't detected any movement, scent or sound since the drip. But I know it's there. The key to my survival is to not let it know that I know. So I gut the cresty right there in the water, letting the river carry away the blood and undesirable organs. This also helps me narrow down my list of potential predators. The blood would have sent some into a mindless hunger. But the predator remained silent even as the river carried the copper odor of a fresh kill past its nose.

It could be another cresty, I think. They don't eat their own kind. Not that I've seen anyway. But it would have to be another small specimen. The stalagmites couldn't possibly hide a large cresty.

Of course, it could be something new. Every time I think I've got a handle on the strange creatures living underground, I run into something new. This might be one such occasion. And if that's the case, I'll need to be extra careful.

With the dead crusty ready for butchering, I drag it to the shore. I pull it half way behind the largest stalagmite I can find, leaving the lower body still visible from the river, but hiding the upper torso, and my body from view. I cut into the dinosaur, making sure the tear of skin is loud. The cut tells the hunter that my attention is on the kill, that this is a good time to strike.

This is not at all true. In fact, I have never been so focused on the world around me. The river fills the cavern with a ceaseless bubbling. The air is clean, but tinged with a mineral scent. The breeze, carried by the water, tickles my skin. There is no sign of the hunter. And this is the moment most creatures in the underworld would shrug their shoulders and return to their meal, only to become a meal themselves a moment later.

Not me. I slide in the dark maze of stalagmites, working my way quickly upriver, then across the water, shifting from one stone pillar to the next like a monkey in the Amazon. In complete silence, I work my way downstream, cross the river again and come up behind the hunter.

I'm downwind. I'm silent. I'm home. A smile creeps onto my face. Whatever predator I'll find has been down here longer than me. It has most likely evolved to life in the underworld. I've been here just over a year, and I've got the thing beat.

I close in slowly. The hunter is still hidden from me. But I find it right where I expected it to be. The thing is concealed in shadow, crouching low, but it is approaching my kill, ready to pounce.

The distance between us is less than ten feet. Two leaps from stalagmite to shore will close the distance in silence. And then, Whipsnap will finish the job. I picture my movements like I do before any kill. One leap. Then another. In the air I'll flex Whipsnap in my hands and upon landing, will let the mace spring loose and sweep out the predator's legs. Once it's down, the spear tip will finish it off.

Had the hunter turned around it would have seen my white teeth spread in a smile. But it didn't turn.

I leap once. Then again.

Whipsnap bends. And snaps!

I hear a roar of pain as Whipsnap sweeps its legs. The creature falls back. A cough escapes its lungs as the air is knocked from them. I pull the spear back, lining up my strike, aiming for the thing's core. My muscles tense, ready to thrust the spear home.

"Wait!" the hunter screams. The voice rolls down the Deep River cavern. I pause, which is strictly against my rules of engagement, and had the voice been any other, I would have struck. But I recognize this voice. It disarms me.

"Ninnis?" I ask.

"Help me up, Ull." A hand emerges from the shadow.

I take hold and pull my mentor to his feet. Despite being dead and nearly killed again, his smile is infectious.

"Well done," he says.

I eye him up and down suspiciously. There is no hugged greeting. No cheerful reunion. I am a hunter now. "I thought you died."

"I know. But it takes more than a little snow to kill old Ninnis." He leans against a stalagmite. "Not that it didn't take its pound of flesh." He holds up his left hand. His pinkie and ring finger are missing. "Frostbite."

I know I should feel some kind of compassion about my friend losing his fingers, but think, *if he'd been faster, he'd still have those fingers.*

He seems to sense my assessment of his injury and gives a nod. He wouldn't be soft on me, either.

"Why didn't you come to me earlier?" I ask.

"This was the first of three tests," he says.

"Surviving on my own?"

"That was part of it, yes. But you also beat me."

"You had to do the same thing when you were trained?"

He nods.

"What happened to your trainer? Is he still alive?"

He laughs. "No, no. I ran him through."

He sees the shift in my gaze and my tightening grip on Whipsnap. He knows what I'm about to do.

"You can kill me if you'd like. I've seen the way you handle that weapon. But it's not necessary."

Our eyes lock. "Why did you kill your trainer?"

"The man was a savage. A brutish relic from the past. He deserved to die. I'd like to think I've done right by you, Ull."

I loosen my grip on Whipsnap. "You have."

"Besides, if you killed me now you might never pass the next two tests."

"Tell me about them. The tests."

He waggles a finger at me. "Later." He eyes my kill. "Right now, I'm famished."

I pull the cresty out from its hiding spot and squat down next to it. If a roast leg commemorating Ninnis's return will loosen his tongue, I'll oblige him. My curiosity over the next two tests has been piqued. Not to mention the long list of questions I have about the creatures and locations I have discovered since he went missing. And if he doesn't answer my questions, well, I might have to unleash a little savagery of my own. Either way, I'll get my answers. But it's nice to have someone to talk to. I would prefer to not have to kill Ninnis yet.

26

"You were watching me the whole time?" I ask Ninnis before taking a bite of the meat I've just prepared over a fire of dried dung. The cresty is tender and juicy like pot roast and I have to slurp the juice from my lower lip after biting it.

"You weren't in eyeshot the entire time." He takes a bite and talks with his mouth full. "That's impossible down here. But I was never more than a few hours behind you, following your tracks, inspecting your kills, gauging your progress. You almost caught me once."

My eyes widen at this revelation. I had no idea Ninnis had survived, let alone remained close by. "When?"

"You found the photo, yes?"

"I did."

"I noticed you were exploring every tunnel and knew you'd

head toward the surface. I was leaving the photo behind, when you returned."

"Where did you hide? I didn't see any cracks or tunnels above that spot."

Picking his teeth, Ninnis reveals, "I was outside. Above you. Be glad you never looked up or your test would have come early."

Before I can ask what he means by that, he asks, "What did you do with the photo?"

"Destroyed it," I say. The lie comes easily. I see no reason to tell him I kept the image. I still don't know why I did it, but I think telling the truth will somehow fail one of his tests.

"Why?"

"The image revolted me." This, at least, is the truth.

"You didn't recognize the people?"

"Should I have? Who were they?"

"Relics from your past, but you'll never see them again."

"Good," I say, tossing my meat to the ground, my appetite sapped by the memory of the two smiling faces. "Why did you expose yourself?"

After a good burp, Ninnis rubs his stomach and says, "It wasn't my intention to expose myself."

I squint at him, suspecting the truth before he confirms it.

"I was to kill you."

"But you failed."

He nods. "And you passed."

I sit straighter, puffing out my chest.

"Don't get cocky, boy. Besting me was a simple thing compared to what comes next. You'll lose the next fight you're in.

There is no way around that."

This news deflates me, and I can hear the truth of it in Ninnis's voice. He's not trying to frighten me. There's a look in his eyes, too, like he's remembering his own test.

"Then what's the point?" I ask.

"The test isn't about winning. It's about how you lose. There are only two possible outcomes. You'll die, or you'll be broken."

"Broken?"

"You remember your first days with me?"

I remember the dog days well. Ninnis's commands were like the very word of God to me. My obedience was unquestionable. "I do."

"But you are not that frail boy anymore. You are Ull, the hunter. Confident. Skilled. But obedient? Not anymore."

I cross my arms. "You haven't asked me to do anything."

He lets out a soft chuckle. "One look in your eyes says you're more likely to gut me for asking anything of you than to obey. That will change tomorrow, but it won't be my voice that commands you. It will be your master's."

I pick up a cresty leg bone that's been picked clean and play with it in my hands. "My master... What can you tell me about him?"

"You tell me," Ninnis says. "You've already met him."

My stomach clutches. I nearly regurgitate my meal. "The giant." The words escape my mouth like a gasp. "At the temple."

"We call it, New Jericho," Ninnis says with a nod. "As a reminder."

"A reminder?"

"Of the treachery of man."

"Who is he?" I say, unable to hide the quiver in my voice.

"It's good that you're afraid," he says. "Shows you still have some common sense left. You might just survive the breaking."

I lean forward, anger filling my eyes and bunching my muscles. "Ninnis, who is he?"

The old man actually relaxes under my harsh gaze. He leans back. "Your master is your namesake."

My nose crinkles. This makes no sense. "Ull? How can I meet myself or be my own master?"

The question sends Ninnis into a fit of laughter. I wait it out as patiently as possible, realizing that he was speaking of the giant. A giant who shares my name. Ull. Norse God of the hunt.

Norse God of the hunt!

I launch to my feet. "Ull is *real?*

Still snickering, Ninnis says, "All the ancient gods are real, though they are not gods in the sense that men believed them to be. They are certainly godlike, having supernatural fathers and human mothers, but they are not all powerful creators. Some would have you believe as much, but it's just not true. They are, however, our superiors in every way. And they're nearly as old as mankind. Our half-brothers.

"At first, we worshiped them. Their size and strength set them apart and above us. They were the heroes of old."

"The men of renown," I add.

He gives me a hard stare. "How do you know these words?"

I shrug. "I don't know. I've retained a lot of information despite having no memory of where or when I learned anything."

He accepts the answer and continues. "Despite their heroic feats, mankind turned against them. With numbers too great to count, a flood of humanity forced the masters underground, long before this continent lay at the bottom of the world. And then the world shifted and Antarctica froze over, trapping the masters here, where they wait for a thaw, and freedom."

"Why don't they wage war on the surface?" I ask.

"They will," Ninnis says. "When their leader returns."

"When will that be?"

Ninnis shrugs. "I don't know. But I suspect you will have something to do with it."

"Me?"

"You are a child of Antarctica. The first and only human child born on the continent in thousands of years, since before the shift. Their magic—they call it spirit—courses through Antarctica to the core. The creatures you've seen. The gigantic caverns. This whole world couldn't exist without it. And when you were born, some of that spirit merged with you. The moment you returned, they knew, and I was sent to bring you home."

This was all fascinating, but my mind has wandered back to my impending meeting with the true Ull. "Then he can't kill me."

"Oh, he rightly can," he says. "And will without hesitation if he thinks they have misjudged you. And you have a lot of ground to make up."

"What do you mean?"

"You didn't make a good first impression."

I remember my meeting with the giant (Ull) at the temple (New Jericho). I had been terrified. Confused. Unhinged. I frown at the memory of his laugh. The deep bellow had permeated my core. And I must face that laugh again. Tomorrow.

My hunter's instincts return. Before any successful hunt, I must rest. My intellect wants to spend the night asking Ninnis questions, but my instincts tell me to sleep because tomorrow I will face death, and if I'm to die I want to do it well rested.

"Then I will make a better second impression," I say before lying back and closing my eyes.

I hear Ninnis laugh again. "And how will you do that?"

"Simple," I say. "I will draw first blood."

27

Five minutes after waking, we start walking. And we keep walking. For hours. Then we're squeezing, climbing and swimming. All in silence. Ninnis's attention is on the journey and all the potential threats along the way. I focus on these things as well, but I'm also thinking about what will happen when we reach our destination.

Ninnis claims to not know our destination, only that we must enter the master's territory. Once there, he'll find us.

Some time ago, we crossed the border of my mental map and entered the unknown. I've been extending the map in my mind, but for any other purpose than backtracking, it's useless without exploring the side tunnels. I make note of all the tunnels, cracks and crevices we pass, along with rivers, bodies of water, pitfalls and other important markers, but I'm not sure if I'll ever return.

I think that's what bothers me. I hate not knowing. It must be some kind of core personality trait because the less I know about this day, the more I'm consumed with irritation.

Ninnis's hand slaps against my shoulder. He's ducked behind a boulder at the end of the tunnel. The space beyond is hidden from view, but the ceiling is vast. He spins back to me and hisses. When danger is near, this is his way of saying, "Shut-up and stay put."

But as he observed the night before, I'm no longer subservient to him. I sniff the air. It's a cresty. I look at Ninnis and feel sorry for him. The scent of cresty blood in easy to detect. The dinosaur is injured. And close. There is nothing to fear.

I leap over Ninnis, Whipsnap held high, and land on the boulder. I scramble silently up the stone. Near the top, I crouch on my feet, preparing to leap out and attack. The size of the cresty doesn't matter. If it's injured, it will fall as easily as a pup. I glance back at Ninnis, who is now up and smiling, and charge over the boulder.

As I move, something about Ninnis's smile strikes me. It's so subtle I nearly miss it. And it's not so much in the shape of his mouth but in the shape of his eyes. A little pinch of his crow's feet that says I'm about to learn a lesson.

Look before you leap, I think.

And I do.

And nearly too late. But I've managed to stop myself just as the blade of an axe bigger than my body whooshes up from below. Had I jumped out as planned I would have been cut in two.

The giant stands. He's monstrous.

His red hair extends from his head down to a full beard that is braided and decorated with human skulls. A large cresty head rests on his head, just above a thick band of gold covering his forehead. The cresty head is attached to a skin hanging down behind him like a cape, containing a quiver of arrows the size of a pole vaulter's pole. He holds a massive bow in one hand and the axe in the other. His red haired chest is bare. His upper arms are adorned in gold bands, and cresty skin gauntlets cover his forearms. He wears tall, brown, soft-soled boots. A gold-buckled belt holds up a brown-scaled skirt.

He is every bit the giant god-man you'd expect...if you could fathom such a thing. Before this moment, I'd thought I could. I'd seen his back side before, though dressed differently. But nothing could prepare me for this monstrous form.

I look at Whipsnap. My weapon is pitiful. I steal a glance at my pale body. The physical prowess I've earned during my time underground seems wholly inadequate.

For a moment I wonder if submission is the point of this test. To acknowledge his superiority over me. Pledge my allegiance to him.

As he notches an arrow (I didn't even see him attach the axe to his belt, but there it is) I know this is wrong. Everything Ninnis taught me has led to this point and the biggest lesson he has taught me is ruthlessness. Ull will be no different. And I can't be either.

I focus on the bow. The string goes taut. The silver tip of the arrow fades from view as it lines up with the spot between my eyes. This is when I act, arching back as far as I can without falling over. I see the giant arrow pass over my face. I feel the tickle of its large feathers against my stomach.

Then I'm up again, and just in time. The axe is back out and crashing down toward me. I dive to the side. Bits of stone shrapnel sting my back as the boulder explodes under the blow.

I hit the stone floor in the massive chamber and roll. A quick glance at my surroundings reveals an arena of sorts. The ceiling is perhaps a hundred feet high. The circular space—not a natural formation—is perhaps three hundred feet across. And all around us are the faces of ancient gods, some of which I recognize, carved into the walls. The Egytian gods: Set, Anubis, Isis and Osiris are the easiest to recognize. Some look South American. Others are clearly Norse. There are Roman gods. Sumerian. Asian. Deities from all of the world's mythologies are represented.

But I have no time to dwell on these things. There is only time to run. Which I do.

The laugh pursues me again.

But this time I don't feel its effect.

Instead, I work out a plan. I told Ninnis I would draw first blood, and that's precisely what I intend to do. I just need to get something out of my pack.

I expect to hear the pounding footfalls of Ull behind me, but he's not giving chase. That's when I remember the bow. I look back and see my death approaching. A burst of fear grips me, but a sudden wind throws off the arrow's trajectory. The projectile passes over my back and buries itself in the solid stone wall on the other end of the arena.

I return my attention to my pack as Ull roars in frustration. I resist the urge to taunt the giant. I need him to think I'm fleeing.

I grip my thirty foot braided skin rope and take it from the pack, which I then drop to the ground. Still running, I place the loop over my shoulder and find the end weighted with a dense stone. As I reach the far end of the arena, I turn and find Ull taking aim once more. He fires. I duck left as a second gust of wind comes and the arrow slams into the wall behind me. When I stand up again, I realize the shot would have been off even if I hadn't moved. Given the renewed roar of frustration coming from the giant, I guess he's not accustomed to missing.

But he's not going to give up. And I need him closer. Much closer. As he nocks a fourth arrow, I pull myself up on to the third arrow, stand atop it, look back and give Ull a cocky little wave of thanks before taking to the wall like a spider.

The effect is immediate. The giant throws down his bow and arrow, takes up the axe again, and charges. As he thunders across the arena, the cresty headdress and cape falls away, exposing the gold ring on his forehead. Seeing the ring on its own struck me as odd. It wasn't decorative. In fact, unlike the rest of Ull's garb, it looked a little silly and out of place. It must have some other significance, I think, and decide to add it to my list of targets—after I draw first blood.

My climb ends when I reach the long snouted carving of Anubis. I stand on the forehead and loose my rope.

Ull is halfway to me. I have just seconds to act.

I spin the line and throw it out. I see the weighted end wrap around the tusk of a god-head I don't recognize. I would normally test the line and make sure it's secure. But I don't have that luxury. Ull, and his axe, are upon me. I leap out and away as the axe comes down. Shards of stone once again pound my back, but I swing away quickly, one hand on the braided line, the other clutching Whipsnap.

As my swing arcs down and away from Ull I think about the arrows that nearly killed me. I would like to say I dodged them on my own, but I don't think that's the case. In both circumstances I felt a gust of wind strike just as I flinched. A theory comes together in my mind and I think back. When I fought and killed the cresty, a gush of water aided me. When Ninnis was nearly killed by an avalanche, I felt strong emotions—emotions I fought to bury. A hundred smaller examples fill my memory as my swing reaches its apex. Bursts of wind. A surge of water. A cloud of snow. All seemingly in response to my emotions and reactions.

Ninnis said Antartica was infused with the magic—with the spirit—of the masters, and being born here, I was too. Maybe that magic somehow bonded me to the land, water and air?

As I swing back toward Ull, I decide to test the theory. It's probably the worst time in history to try something like this. It might get me killed. But I can't resist.

I had planned to let go at the base of my return swing and plunge my spear tip into Ull's foot, quickly do whatever damage I could to slow him down and then keep moving. My new plan is much more direct.

The return swing takes me back to where the head of Anubis

used to be (it's a heap of stone on the arena floor now). A cloud of stone dust fills the space between Ull and me, which is convenient because it keeps him from swatting me out of the air like a fly. And when I let go of the rope at the apex of my swing and take to the air, that's as close an approximation of what I am to the giant as I can conceive. I am a bug in his sight.

But I pack a nasty sting.

Putting my theory to the test, I wish with all my being that I would be carried higher. The request isn't forced or phony. If I fall, I'll die. For a moment, I start to fall, but the sinking in my stomach, churns a surge of emotion through my body and a gust of wind catches me and carries me higher, straight toward Ull's head.

The dust parts for me. I emerge from it and let out a howl. Ull turns toward me, the briefest look of surprise in his black eyes. Then his confidence returns, but only for a moment. I see his eyes reflect fear. I unleash Whipsnap, striking an upward blow to the golden ring surrounding his large head. There is a clang of stone on metal. The ring springs free from his head and flips away.

I sense several things that mark a change in this encounter. First is Ull's brief fear. Second is Ninnis's gasp, audible all the way across the arena. Third is the pulse I see beneath Ull's forehead. It's a soft spot. And Ull is hardly human. Whatever it is, it must be vital.

I twist as I fall, facing Ull's body. I stab out with Whipsnap. I merely meant to impale the scaled leather skirt and slow my fall, but I pass the skirt and stab deep into the meat above his knee. The spear tip catches and I slam into his booted shin.

The tip comes loose and I fall the rest of the way to the stone floor.

Ull steps back, glancing down at his bleeding leg while testing his bare head with his other hand, searching for the missing metal ring. He's not holding his axe. He's paying no attention to me. This is my chance.

I get to my feet, take aim with Whipsnap and let the spear fly.

A moment later, it plunges deep into Ull's flesh.

28

Ull lowers his hand. He had raised it at the last moment, allowing the spear-tipped end of Whipsnap to pierce his hand, rather than his forehead. I stand there, stunned, as the giant looks at the weapon buried in his hand and smiles. His teeth are yellow and sharp. When he lets out a laugh I see multiple rows of teeth, just like the egg-monsters.

He turns his eyes on me and holds out his wounded hand. With his other hand, he takes the spear and pulls it slowly out of his flesh. Blood drips as my weapon slurps out of his hand. The blade bites for a moment, but he tugs at it quickly and the whole thing comes free.

He tosses Whipsnap aside like it's a used-up matchstick and holds the wound out for me to see. Blood oozes from the hole in his hand for just a moment. Then as quickly as Whipsnap pierced his hand, the wound seals over and disappears.

A shudder runs through Ull's body. His smile widens. And his eyes are back on me. "Pain is delightful, don't you think?" The deep bass of his voice shakes my insides.

For a moment, I wonder how it is this ancient man-monster can speak English, but decide it is one of the least perplexing things about this world. Ninnis could have easily taught him the language.

When Ull takes a step toward me, cutting the distance between us in half, I know there is nowhere I can run. With no weapon, I have no defense. My only consolation is that he's not nocking an arrow or wielding the axe. But when his arm reaches back, I know he's going to strike me.

I could run and might avoid his reach for a time. I might even make it to Whipsnap.

But what he has just shown me makes the effort useless. Ninnis told me that this was a fight I could not win. And he's right. Killing Ull would be impossible.

As the swing descends I think I should try to relax my body as tense limbs can't flex and break more easily. But no matter how hard I will myself to stay limber, my muscles cramp up with a sudden twitch.

Two things run through my mind before the blow connects.

This is going to hurt.

And, *if he's not trying to kill me now, I passed!*

A grin spreads on my lips a moment before he sends me flying. I feel my arm and several ribs break. I see the floor passing beneath me. There goes Whipsnap. How far did he hit me? I spin round and see the stone floor of the cavern rising up to meet me. Landing may hurt more than being hit, and my insides cringe. With the twist of fear comes a burst of wind. It doesn't stop me, but it certainly slows me down.

I hit the stone, roll for several feet and then slide to a stop on my back.

The pounding of Ull's feet is hard to ignore, even with my body screaming out in pain. I turn toward him, wondering if he's done. The look in his eyes says he's not.

So I stand to face him again.

There is no pause when he arrives. He simply strikes me and sends me flying. I land near the entrance.

I think both arms are broken now, but my legs are fine. It's hard to say, as I feel the pain from my wounds from head to toe. I turn and see Ninnis's feet nearby.

Then Ull is pounding toward me again.

I sit up and try to stand. It's harder without my arms.

"Stay down, you fool!" Ninnis hisses at me.

But I won't stay down. My body may be broken, but my will isn't. And I know what I want. Ull has revealed the true nature of the spirit living in me.

Anger. Hate. Pain.

I crave it.

It fuels me.

I spit blood at Ninnis's feet and face my master.

Ull stops above me, pausing. I can feel my face swelling and I'm sure he can see it. I smell my blood seeping from countless wounds. My arms dangle uselessly. I am beaten. I am broken.

I look up at him, meeting his eyes.

My body wobbles. I giggle. The funniest quote has entered my mind. I don't know what it's from, but I know it's funny and I speak it aloud. Mimicking Ninnis's proper accent, I say, "Please sir, can I have some more?"

Then I laugh hysterically.

The last thing I remember about this day is Ull saying, "You have earned the use of my name today, little Ull."

Then he honors my request, and gives me more.

29

After a long time not feeling hot or cold, the burning that courses through my body upon waking makes me scream. Ninnis is above me a moment later. I can't hear his words over the pain, but his open palms are urging me to stop.

I see my arms then, flailing like wounded fish, splashing something red that could be my blood, but looks more like fruit punch. I focus on my arms and stop them.

But I'm still screaming.

Ninnis is right above me now. He's enunciating very clearly and though I can't hear his voice over my own, I can read his lips.

"Calm down," he says. "It hurts less if you don't fight it."

I try. I try my best. And reduce the scream to a whimper.

But the pain is so intense, permeating me to the core, that I think bottling it up completely might make me explode.

"What's happening?" I manage to squeak out.

"You're being healed," he says. "The technique is typically used on a limb or wound, but your whole body was broken. You almost died. We had to immerse you."

I manage a look down. I'm lying in what I can only describe as a stone tub. It's full of watery red liquid. "What is it?"

"Ull's blood diluted with water. Straight blood would kill you."

"Feels like it's killing me."

"If we left you in there, it would. In fact, if you hadn't been born here, I think it would have already. But you seem to have a little bit of their blood in you already."

I give a weak nod. "The spirit of the Nephilim."

Ninnis leans in closer. "Where did you hear that name?"

It's hard to focus on an answer, mostly because I don't know, and that's what I tell him.

He stares at me. I can tell he doesn't believe me.

Then it comes to me. "Heroes of old. Men of renown. There were Nephilim on the Earth in those days, and I am like a grasshopper in their sight."

I know I'm paraphrasing. Probably butchering whatever it is I'm quoting. But my mind has put together some puzzle pieces. "I must have read it somewhere before I came here." I can see Ninnis believes me now. "Is that right? Are our masters the Nephilim?"

He nods. "They are."

My head spins, but I don't think the cause is the revelation of my master's identity. The pain is dulling, or my consciousness is fading. I feel my heart skip a beat. "How will you know when to take me out?" I ask, but it comes out garbled. The brown stone room swirls around me.

I feel my head lull back as my vision fades.

Ninnis says, "That's how I know." And I feel his arms slide under me. Then nothing.

* * *

When I open my eyes again, I no longer feel pain. In fact, I'm positively comfortable. I'm lying on my side and can see the gray skin of an egg-monster beneath me. Actually, it must be a stack of skins, because when I shift my weight, the cushion conforms to my body. Two soft skins cover me like blankets. Since my life underground began, I've slept without cover. The weight feels good.

For a moment, I think I will drift back to sleep, but I force myself up as memories of my bloody baptism return. I remove the blankets and inspect my body. My wounds are healed. I move my arms. They work without a hitch. I take a deep breath. There is no pain, so my ribs must be healed, too.

I slide out of the bed and stand. My balance is good. A few good leaps confirm my legs are strong. I fall forward like a tree cut by Ull's axe and catch myself just inches from the stone floor. Strong as ever.

Hopping back to my feet, I inspect the room. The brown stone walls are similar to what I saw from the tub, but are covered in graffiti. Swirls, circles and intersecting lines. The symbols look vaguely familiar, like those on the obelisks from New Jericho. Hanging from a hook next to the bed (which, as I suspected, is made from a stack of at least thirty eggy skins) is a cresty head and cloak that matches Ull's. I try it on.

The teeth are sharp and bite into my forehead. But I don't mind, the pain feels good and the grip helps it stay on. The cloak hangs over my shoulders and stops just before the floor. I wish I had a mirror.

"It suits you," Ninnis says from the doorway.

I turn toward him and find him dressed in black leathers, though much of his body is still bare. He notices my inquisitive look. "When we are in one of the citadels, we are to dress as our masters do. It's a sign of respect, but it also protects you."

"Protects me?"

"From the others. Until you are branded, the cloak marks you as the property of Ull, son of Thor, son of Odin. A strong blood-line that the others will not dare violate. If you misstep and re-quire punishment, it will be handled by your master, or your master's brethren alone. The Norse will not go lightly on you, but they won't kill you either. Certainly not after the promise you showed in the arena."

I brighten at his words. "I did well?"

"You did exceptional. In fact, I have never heard of one of the masters being wounded in the trial. Ull is quite proud. He has spread word of your deeds across the continent over the past month."

"A month? I've been unconscious for a month?"

"Roughly. I think. Thirty wakings and sleepings. That's how you keep track of time, yes?"

I'm not sure I ever told him as much, but he had watched me for quite a while. It's possible he figured it out.

"My injuries took that long to heal?"

"Your wounds were healed the moment I took you out of the bath. But the effect of the master's blood on the mind is powerful. And your exposure was intense. How do you feel?"

"Never better."

"Good," he says. "Your final test is tomorrow and while it will not be as painful as the last, it will require all of your skills. When you pass that test, this room will be yours along with one like it in all the citadels. You will be part of the Norse house and receive all of the benefits of the bloodline."

"When will I be branded?"

Ninnis sits on the bed and tests the cushion. "You won't be."

"Why not?"

"You will belong to the Norse for a time, but once you are prepared for the task, body and soul, you will offer yourself up to another."

"Not given?"

"No," Ninnis says. "You must give yourself over to him willingly."

"Give myself to who?"

He ponders answering for a moment, then shakes his head. "You have earned the truth. Or at least the small part I dare reveal. You will give yourself to the very first master. He is the oldest and strongest of them, and they are all named for him. Nephil, father of Enlil and Enki, who is my master and ruler of this world."

"Is he here now?" I ask eagerly. "Can I meet him now?"

Ninnis frowns and looks to the floor. "He is not here. He has not been among us for a very long time."

"Where is he?"

He continues staring at the floor, like he can see straight through it. "Below us. In Tartarus."

Tartarus. "I thought that was a Greek version of hell?"

"Tartarus predates the Greeks. It is a physical realm, unlike hell, and is far worse. He is a prisoner there. His spirit is trapped. Unable to escape until bonded with a body strong enough to enter Tartarus and return."

My eyes grow wide. "They think I can do this?"

Ninnis stands. "I've said too much."

"But—"

"Speak of this to no one," he says. "You will be told everything when the time is right."

"Ninnis, please," I persist, but that just fuels his anger.

"Quiet, Ull! You best focus yourself on the final test! Eat. Regain your strength and wit. If you fail tomorrow you will learn nothing more than what hell awaits you in the afterlife as you are torn limb from limb. You have earned a place of honor here. See that you retain it!"

I bow my head, acknowledging his wisdom. "What is the final trial?"

"A hunt. On the surface."

My heart races with anticipation. My sleeping body missed the hunt.

"And our prey?"

Ninnis grins now, his anger erased. "The best kind. Human."

30

I haven't slept again by the time Ninnis comes back, but I have eaten, three times. I'm not sure who brings the food, but every so often there is a knock on the wooden door. When I answer it, there is a plate of cooked meat on the hallway floor. It is the best food I've eaten since I can remember, but there is no one to thank for it.

Though I've been in the room for hours, I haven't ventured more than a few feet past the door. The hallway dwarfs my room, which is closer to a mouse hole by comparison. I'm not sure, but this must be some kind of human-only portion of the citadel. The doors lining both sides of the hallway are all human sized despite the space being large enough for two Nephilim walking side by side.

Most of the doors are open and the rooms beyond are empty. I suspect that they belong to other hunters, like Ninnis—like me—who are in other parts of the continent right now. I wish I could meet them now, but suspect I will after I pass this third and final test.

I lie on the egg-monster skin bed and stare at the ceiling. But I'm no longer seeing its graffiti-covered surface. Instead, I picture as many different scenarios as possible. I know I'll be on the surface, so there will likely be snow on the ground. Maybe cracks in the ice to hide in. If I'm lucky it will be night, but I suspect it will be day. The darkness of night would make things too easy.

It will be daylight. I'm sure of it. And the sun will hurt my eyes. In fact, with the surface of Antarctica largely barren of cover and either stripped clean by high winds or covered in snow, hiding may well be impossible. My white skin will help me blend in with the snow and ice. But my hair—I take a handful of the clumpy red mass and pull it in front of my eyes—my hair will stand out like a beacon.

The odds are against me being stealthy. But maybe that's not required? Before I can picture a thousand ways to charge at and quickly kill another human being, Ninnis is at the door.

"It's time," he says.

The journey is several miles of uphill paths. Ull accompanies us most of the way and sets our pace at a brisk walk—for him. Ninnis and I have to run to keep up and when the terrain gets rough, that becomes a challenge for both of us. Several hours later we reach the end of our journey. The forty foot tall tunnel shrinks down to ten and Ull stops.

"This is where we part ways, little Ull," he says. "I will wait here for your return and the report of your success or failure."

I nod.

"Should you succeed, you will be welcome in the halls of Asgard for the rest of your days."

"Asgard?" I ask.

"The citadels," Ninnis says. "Asgard. Olympus. Tuat. They're the dwelling places of the masters."

"I—I know," I say. "I just never thought they were—"

"Real?" Ull finishes. He leans in close, his head larger than my body. "We are very real, little hunter." He motions for the small tunnel ahead. "Now go. And do not fail."

"I won't," I say before heading into the tunnel with Ninnis.

After another mile hike, we reach the end of the tunnel. A wall of glowing white caps the end. I squint at the bright sphere of snow.

Ninnis dons a pair of sunglasses.

"None for me?" I ask.

"Not this time," he says. "No weapons. No gear. Just this."

He holds up a leather bag.

"What's this for?"

"Several hundred feet below the exit you will find a man and a woman. Put this over her head and capture her, alive."

I take it. "And the man? Can I kill him?"

"No," he says. "The point of this test is subtlety and control. The outside world can't know we're here until we are ready to reveal ourselves. He must believe her disappearance to be an accident or result of some natural phenomenon. *You* got lost in a

storm. I fell into a fissure. And we were both left for dead as a result."

I understand and head for the snowy wall. For a moment I
think I'll have to dig through, but a small opening on the left reveals a sliver of blue sky. I slide through the narrow opening and
find my eyes assaulted.

I adjust to the light slowly, but after several minutes I can open
my eyes enough to see the world around me. The mountain
slopes down and splits into a valley, barren of snow, far below us.
In the valley, two people kneel by what looks like a large, partially
uncovered limb. I can't make out what they're doing, but I suspect the woman is the one dressed in bright pink. I can't remember why, but pink feels like a feminine color to me. The man is
wearing bright orange.

I step out into the day and Ninnis takes my arm. "Take as long
as you need. If you're detected, you fail. If they escape, you fail. If
you resort to violence, you fail. Understand?"

"I do," I say, pulling away.

"I'll be watching," he says, holding up a pair of binoculars.

I put the leather bag over the top of my head and stuff my hair
up inside. Ninnis gives me a worried look, like I've lost my mind.
I know I must look ridiculous, but my plan will work. "If they see
me, they'll see a brown rock on the white snow."

He smiles. "We'll see about that."

I lie down on the snow, feeling the powder melt beneath my
warmth, but feeling no cold in return. "Be back soon." I pull my

self across the snow, sliding on my stomach and begin a slow descent toward my unsuspecting prey.

31

It takes me two hours to slide down the mountainside. It's not hard work—my body heat melts the top layer of snow, making it slick beneath me, and I can't feel the cold—but I'm careful. My targets' attention is mostly on the ground and whatever it is they're working on. But occasionally one of them will look up. I am perfectly camouflaged with my white skin and hidden hair. But it's possible one of them could notice the brown rock/bag covering my head is moving slowly toward them. They're probably admiring the view, which is impressive, even through my squinted eyes.

My thoughts turn to Antarctica. It's a magical land deserving of admiration, possibly even worship. They're right to admire it. But it's *my* land. I am bonded to it and it to me. No one has told me this, but I can feel it.

And I can prove it scientifically.

I pause there in the snow, exposed but invisible, and apply some scientific method. I'm not sure why I know this, or why I feel it's important, but I know it will erase my doubts, and if true, will help my current situation.

Step one. Ask a question. Am I bonded to Antarctica and its environment below the surface, on the surface and...in the atmosphere?

Step two. Background research. I've already done this. I've experienced several examples of my emotions and strong reactions creating an environmental response. I'm also impervious to the effects of the environment. I don't just not feel cold, it actually does no harm to my body. No reddening skin. No frostbite.

Step three. Construct a hypothesis. According to Ninnis, when I was born on Antarctica, its spirit, created by Nephilim magic (or something supernatural) was channeled into my body. Ninnis claimed it made me part Nephilim. As much as I'd like that, I don't agree. I think it bonded me with the continent. The Nephilim made this land a living thing and when I was bonded to it, they gave it a brain—albeit, unknowingly. That's my hypothesis.

Step four. Test with an experiment. I've been debating what this should be. Something subtle, that only I will notice.

I check my targets. They're hard at work. With my eyes trained on them, I slowly roll onto my back. Subtle, I think, then focus my mind and emotions on a single event.

It's only thirty seconds before I see it above me, fluttering down from above. The tiny snowflake descends above my face and lands on the tip of my nose. My hypothesis is true. I repeat the test to be sure, this time bringing five flakes down. When they touch down on the tip of my nose and melt, I focus on the resulting bead of water. It doesn't run off to either side, or roll toward my forehead as it should (I'm laying downhill). Instead, it does as I will it, evaporating back into the atmosphere.

I fight the intense urge to laugh, and realize my elation might make me sloppy. I have a task to finish and Ninnis is probably wondering why I'm just lying here. For some reason, I don't want him to know what I can do. Not yet. If they know that I'm different, that I'm strange, they may not welcome me. They may not allow me to offer myself to Nephil. I just can't risk that yet.

So I turn myself over and stalk my prey.

I can hear their voices now, filtering up out of the valley. They're deep in conversation.

I take a chance, thrusting myself hard. My body slides over the snow, building speed as I descend. I travel a distance that would have taken an hour to cover at my previous pace, in thirty seconds. As I approach the valley, I make a show of putting my hands on the snow to stop. But this is not what stops me. A burst of wind, like that katabatic in reverse, skims across the snowy slope and slows me to a silent stop.

I pull myself behind a rocky outcrop at the top of the valley wall. I can see them below. It looks like they're digging a bone from the ice. I recognize the limb as a cresty femur, but this one is old. Fossilized.

If they only knew much fresher specimens still lived beneath their feet.

A quick survey of the valley shows very little cover to hide behind. And the trip back up, with the woman in tow, will be slow. For a moment, I wonder if they want me to fail. Or maybe it's just Ninnis. Did he devise this test? When I succeed, will he be disappointed?

And I will succeed. There is no doubt about that.

My first task is finding an escape route that doesn't require me dragging the bright pink clad woman all the way back up the mountain. I turn my attention to the valley, searching for cracks or fissures that may lead underground. *Where are you?* I think. *Show yourself.*

A puff of dusty air rises from behind a boulder. I can't see it, but I know its there. I can feel it now.

Now to address the issue of concealment.

With my head lowered and eyes closed, I create a storm inside me. I see it building like a dark monster, swirling with anger. I see an army of thick snow flakes carried by intense wind. It pours out of me.

My eyes snap open. I'm exhausted. Barely able to move.

What's happening to me? I think.

Then a shadow falls over me. Then the valley. I don't bother turning around. I know what's there, blotting out the sun. When the first flake of snow arrives, I grin and feel a measure of energy return. But it's barely enough to move, let alone strike.

I hear the voices below, engaged in a conversation tinged with sarcasm, but I can't make out the words. But a moment later, the man turns in my direction and I can hear exactly what he says. "My... Where'd that come from?"

She says something. His name I think. And then he's shouting and grabbing a blue tarp. "Wrap up the fossil! I'll get the other side. Fasten it tight!"

"There isn't time!" she shouts, and she's right. The snow and wind descend over them like a crashing wave.

The world turns white. Judging by their shouts, they've lost each other in the whiteout. I stand without fear of being seen and enter the valley. As adrenaline rushes into my body, my energy returns. I can't see the woman, but her cries for help are like a lighthouse beacon. As I run toward her, my emotions soar. I feel the wind kick up behind me, pushing me forward, and when I can no longer contain my excitement I let out a howl. My voice mixes with the rushing wind as my soul mixes with the land.

I remove the hood from my head, unleashing my long red hair. A flash of bright pink directs me to the woman. I approach from behind and with the quickness of a cobra strike snap the hood over her head. I plant my hand over her hooded mouth, stifling her cry to a dull, "Hmph!"

She fights for a moment, but a quick strike to the back of her skull saps her energy. Her legs go out from under her and she falls into my arms. I make for the crack in the valley floor and slide in, dragging the woman behind me. Her thick jacket catches a few times, but the crack opens wide a few feet down, and then we're through.

I want to remove the hood and look into the eyes of my prey, but I'm not sure I should. Not following the test parameters exactly as described might lead to failure. So I leave the hood on and cinch it shut around her neck. I've never been in this tunnel before, but I know the general direction I need to go to find Ninnis again: up.

As I carry the woman deeper, I will the storm to last a few minutes more, long enough for the woman to have conceivably wandered off. Just another victim of Antarctic whiteout conditions.

I find Ninnis about an hour later. He's still at the tunnel exit, scanning the area below with his binoculars. His distraction is so intense that he doesn't hear me approach. I clear my throat.

Ninnis whirls around, ready for a fight, but then sees me.

And then the woman.

He is honestly stunned, but not disappointed like I had worried.

"How did you—I don't—what..." He pauses, shaking his head. "I'm having a hard time believing what I just saw, and what I didn't see, and what I'm seeing now. The storm, it just came and went precisely when you needed it to."

I shrug.

"How did you know?" His voice is growing angry. He suspects I had something to do with it. Maybe he remembers how Ull's arrows somehow kept missing me. Maybe my sudden stop at the bottom of the mountain wasn't convincing. Or maybe it's just the convenient timing of a whiteout storm. But he's starting to suspect.

So I lie. "I felt a cold breeze on my back about halfway down. You saw me roll over?"

He nods slowly.

"I was watching the storm, gauging its speed as it rose up over the mountain. It came in fast, so I slid down in time to take advantage. When it struck, so did I. There was a crack in the valley floor. It led to a tunnel, and here we are."

He stares at me for a moment. A hint of a smile appears.

"Did the man see anything?" I ask.

"See for yourself," Ninnis says, handing me the binoculars. I step outside and look down the mountainside. The man was still in the valley, which was coated with a thin film of snow. He's pacing, hands cupped to his mouth, screaming. He saw nothing. All he knows is that the woman is missing. It's all he'll ever know.

When I re-enter the tunnel, Ninnis is kneeling down next to the woman, checking her pulse. "She's alive," he says before standing up and offering me his hand.

I shake it.

"Congratulations," he says. "You passed in rare form. As seems typical for you."

The woman stirs. Ninnis strikes her without pause and she falls limp again. "Come," he says. "Let's get you back to the citadel and clean you up."

"For what?" I ask.

"Your banquet. I've heard it will be like no other, in honor of Ull the hunter, vessel of Nephil, Lord of the Nephilim."

32

I'm feeling pretty good. Actually, I can't remember ever feeling so happy. So proud. I have overcome the hardest challenges of the underworld. I have joined a people whom I respect, and who will one day worship me. And I have discovered my bond with the land of Antarctica. Despite being the smallest of my kind, I am larger than life. I could see it in the way Ull looked at me when Ninnis related the story of my final test.

When we returned to the citadel, I saw many more Nephilim warriors, some smaller than my master, Ull, some larger. All of them bowed to me as a sign of respect. But I wasn't introduced to any of them—though I see symbols and headdresses that look familiar. I was led back to my quarters, given a bowl of fresh water and told to wash. Which I did.

And now I'm sitting on my bed waiting. I've been waiting so

long I start to think this is really the final test. If it is, I'm about to fail. I stand and turn toward the door. At that moment, there is a knock.

I rush for the door, swing it open and find no one. There is, however, a bundle of clothing on the hallway floor. I scan the giant hall, looking for someone, but find the space empty. Who could hide from me so quickly? It doesn't seem possible.

The clothes are a smaller scale of Ull's. The leather scaled skirt. The gauntlets. And a golden ring for my head. But what holds my attention are the objects lying to the side of the clothing. There is Whipsnap, now polished and sporting a razor sharp metal blade and spiked mace ball, my climbing claws, restrung with fresh leather straps, and my telescope, which I thought lost forever in the New Jericho lake.

I collect the items and retreat to my room. I dress first and find that everything fits perfectly, from the soft soled leather boots to the plain metal crown. I find a satchel attached to my belt, big enough to hold the climbing claws and a pocket that buttons, in which the telescope fits snugly. There are also two clips on the belt. I'm not sure what they're for until I find that Whipsnap fits in them securely. I bent the shaft around my body, clipping the other end in place so that the blade and mace are to my sides, both pointing back. It seems like a silly design to me until I take hold of the weapon and give it a tug. Both ends detach simultaneously. Whipsnap springs out, snapping open in my hands. One second, it's hardly visible around my waist. The next it's in my hand and ready to kill. I'll need to unclip it for tight squeezes, but having my hands free most of the time will be a great help.

After securing Whipsnap to the belt, I don my cresty hood and cloak. I once again long for a mirror and then remember the bowl of water. I place the bowl on the floor and stand over its still surface. The perspective of my reflection makes me look like a giant. Like the great Ull, himself. My garb and red hair, which is a darker red than I remember it being before, complete the illusion.

Looking and feeling like a giant, I can no longer resist leaving my room. I have not been formally welcomed yet, but I know this is my home now. I can go where I please. As I leave my room behind, I decide I won't go far. Though I can go wherever I want, I still do not know my way around and would not want to miss the banquet being prepared in my honor.

I start by inspecting some of the other nearby rooms. Some are completely empty. Others hold weapons and discarded clothing, I assume from other hunters who are somewhere else in the citadel, perhaps tending to the needs of their masters or preparing for the banquet.

I think about who will be there. Ninnis said that at least one member from each of the warrior tribes will be there along with a representative from each class—seekers, thinkers, breeders, feeders, gatherers—along with many of my fellow hunters. I wonder what they'll look like. What they'll sound and smell like. And what will we eat? Will there be new meats to try? Will we dine on roast cresty or egg-monster stew?

As my mouth waters over the possibilities, I notice one of the human-sized doors is closed. Was it open before? I think it was, which means someone might be inside. I head for the door, hoping the person inside will recognize me, bow and show me respect. I just can't get enough of this, which I suppose is good, since I suspect it's a habit that will carry on indefinitely once I accept the spirit of Nephil to live inside me.

Ull confirmed what Ninnis told me about Nephil, but left out many details. "Enki has reserved that honor for himself as Nephil's first son," Ull had explained on the hike back to the citadel. "Your patience will be rewarded."

And it would be. Of that I have no doubt.

But patience is hard to come by when boredom is stacking the odds.

So I knock on the door.

No one answers.

I knock again. When no answer comes a second time, I decide that I not only have the right to wander the halls of Asgard, I also have the right to open doors. I find it unlocked and step inside.

The room is as plain as mine. An egg-monster skin bed. A stone shelf. Little more.

A lump in the corner moves. Shakes, really. Is that a person?

"Hello?" I say.

The body trembles.

I search the room for clues and see a splash of pink just beyond the bed. A quick peek reveals a thick pink jacket. This is the woman I captured. Her lack of response immediately fills me with anger.

"Answer me, woman."

I hear a squeak of sound. Did she speak or simply cry out?

I step closer.

She's dressed in leather rags. Her black hair is tied back in a tight braid. Was it like that when I took her? I wonder, but then remember her head was covered by the jacket's hood. Her skin is dark, darker than anything I've seen underground. Her dark hands cover the side of her face, which is turned into the corner of the room.

"Tell me your name," I say.

Her hands shake.

I clench my fists. "I am the hunter who took you. You will show me respect."

"Why?" she says, her voice a chaotic vibrato.

"Why, what?"

"Why..." She sniffs. "Why did you take me?"

"I do not know why the masters wanted you specifically, but you were my final test."

"Test?"

"To become one of them."

"Who are *they*?"

"They are the sons of Nephil, the Nephilim. The heroes of old. The—"

"Men of renown," she finishes.

This infuriates me. "Who are you?" I shout. "Show me your face!"

Her shaking hands lower. Her cheek bears a fresh wound, perhaps dealt by me, or Ninnis, or after she was brought here. She turns slowly, and then looks up, meeting my eyes.

Her eyes strike me like one of Ull's arrows. I stumble back as her face contorts into something horrible, something sinister, burning with hate. And I feel an emotion I thought I would never experience again.

I am unhinged.

I am terrified.

33

When I strike the hard stone wall, my senses return for a moment. I take hold of Whipsnap and pull. The weapon snaps out. I toss my cresty skin to the side, spin the weapon into position, blade forward, and meet her eyes again.

My mind explodes.

I'm no longer in the room. The woman is gone. Everything is gone.

I am warm and comfortable, surrounded by darkness, and supported on all sides by something soft. Then something disrupts my state of bliss. An intense pressure builds around me. It does not hurt, but it is not comfortable either.

The pressure continues for some time, and I have a feeling of rushing through it.

I'm fast-forwarding through the memory.

Is this a memory?

What's fast-forwarding?

I'm not remembering this. I'm reliving *it.*

Then there is light. And cold. And wetness.

I feel myself being drawn up, away from the warmth.

There is a crackle of sound so crisp and clear that it frightens me. When I scream, a high pitched squeal comes out. The noise that frightened me was my own voice. Everything smells wrong.

That's because I've never smelled before.

There's a tug on my belly. And a pinch. I cry out again. I'm shaking from cold and fright. Confusion grips my thoughts. I can feel myself slipping into hysteria.

Then I see her looking down at me. She's smiling. And her eyes...her eyes!

"No!" I scream, swinging Whipsnap out, intending to sever the woman's throat, but I don't come close.

She stands, pushing herself back into the corner, but never taking her eyes off me. She reaches out a shaking hand.

"Stay back!" I swing again, this time throwing myself off balance. I drop Whipsnap and catch myself on the bed.

She speaks a single word that throws me violently into the past once again. "Solomon."

She's looking down at me, holding me in her hands, wrapping me in something warm. I'm used to warm and wet, but warm and dry is better than cold. And now she's speaking to me. Smiling as she coos my name. "Solomon," she says. "Solomon." Her inflections are soothing. Her white teeth hold my gaze as she speaks. She brings me up close, so close I can feel her warm breath. "You are a precious boy," she says, and then turns me away.

As she turns me I see the room through blurry eyes. But I see shapes I will come to know well and recognize them instantly.

Outside the memory, I shout for them. "Mom! Dad! Where are you?"

The memory of my birth flickers.

The stone room spins around me.

I fall to my knees.

My mind is on fire. Pressure builds around the chink in whatever mental dam has been put in place. Memories come fast, but are really just a quick spray. The first year of my life returns. The dam weakens. Then breaks.

In a single moment, like the explosion of an atomic bomb, thirteen years of perfect memory—nearly seven million minutes of data—slams into my mind at once.

I'm two years old, wearing blue footie pajamas. I'm staying at my grandmother's house with my parents. And I'm entertaining them by standing in the potty-training potty and waving my arms around.

I'm five now. My parents are ice skating, motioning me to follow. I don't have skates on, and the ice is slippery, and I can see flowing water in the distance where the river enters the lake. I know that's bad and I worry about falling through.

Seven. I'm riding my banana seat bike in the driveway. I don't ride in the street anymore. Not since a neighbor got hit by the diaper truck after riding straight out of the driveway. It rained recently. I can smell the water on the warm pavement.

The next three years flash past in a blur of school, playing and being tested. Then I'm in school and the kids are all older than me. I feel very small and afraid. All I can think about is going home, and that's okay because I know all the answers.

Thirteen. I'm sharing pizza with Justin and my parents. There's a volcano for my present. A song about brick houses. And an explosion of red. Then comes the ticket. One of the pivotal moments of my life. I flash to the trip. Dr. Clark is with me, telling me I'm different, and special. And Mirabelle. The nicest girl I ever knew, who managed to steal my heart and image with the click of a Polaroid camera.

The night of my capture returns in detail. Ninnis attacks. I strike Aimee. The generator. Then the pit.

I pitch forward and vomit.

When the contraction ends, I suck in a bile flavored breath.

Then I'm vomiting again. It feels like my organs are sliding out of my throat, like there will be nothing left of myself when I am done. When I realize that is exactly what is happening, I accept it, and wait.

When I'm done I'm surprised to find only a small puddle beneath my mouth. I have not eaten in some time and the majority of my heaves brought up nothing, except, I think, my soul.

When I stand, I am myself again.

I am Solomon.

I bring my eyes up and meet hers once more.

She can see the change in me. In my eyes. In my body language.

I *am* Solomon.

Solomon!

"Solomon," I whisper as though hearing my name for the first time.

She nods. "Solomon."

When I speak her name, my last bit of toughness breaks. "Aimee?"

She reaches out to me with both arms. I rush to her and bury myself in her embrace, weeping for what I've done to her, for the life that I have lived since I last saw her, for thinking—for believing—that the woman who first showed me love was evil. Her arms are strong around me. Her head is pressed on top of mine. And she speaks a sentence that clutches my throat and squeezes, "You are a precious boy."

I have been reborn.

Into her arms once again.

And despite all I have done, all the pain I have caused her, she has loved me first.

Again.

34

My senses return long enough for me to close the door. I can't be seen like this. They might kill us both. Or decide to break me again and steal my memories a second time. Were I still alone, I think I might prefer death to losing myself again, but I now have Aimee to consider.

And I brought her here. *I* brought her here.

With the door closed I sit on the bed and weep silently. Aimee sits next to me and rubs my back. Her affection only makes me cry harder, but I think that's what I need—to pour the vileness out. The tears are purifying.

Thoughts of my father and how we parted fill my thoughts. "My father," I say.

Her hand pauses on my back. "Misses you horribly. As does your mother."

"They believe I'm dead?"

After a pause, she whispers, "Yes. They stayed for a year searching for you."

I remember seeing them now. Looking through the telescope. They looked so sad. A sob escapes my mouth. I know how heartbroken they must have felt. I'm feeling it now.

"You'll see them again," she says confidently, but it's hard to believe.

It's ten minutes before I'm able to speak again. "I'm sorry. For taking you."

"I forgive you," she says with missing a beat.

"Why?"

"You weren't yourself."

This is true, but, "If I had been stronger, this wouldn't have happened."

She turns my face toward hers. Dry white lines streaking over her cheeks from her eyes reveal she's been crying too. "What did they do to you, Sol?"

I relate the story as best I can, concentrating on the important events: the night I was taken, my time in the pit, my first kill, my training, the three tests that ended with her capture. She listens to it all silently, reacting to everything with an array of facial expressions. When I'm done, tears fill her eyes again.

"My poor child," she says, touching my cheek with her hand. "Why? Why did they do all this to you? Who are they?"

"I think you know who they are," I say.

"The men of renown," she guesses.

I nod.

"The Nephilim?" She shakes her head. I can see she thinks it's impossible, but she looks around the room, seeing the reality of things. She can't explain it. "But how?"

I relate the story Ninnis told me. About the Nephilim living among men, how they were worshipped, how they were our heroes, and then how we eventually turned against them and drove them away. "We pushed them underground," I say. "And they've been living here since."

As I relate the story, I feel a stirring of sympathy for my masters.

They're not my masters!

I feel an invisible hand clutch my throat. They still have some hold on me. Like a trapdoor spider, everything they turned me into is waiting for my guard to drop. Then it will strike out, fill me with poison and consume my soul again. Ull, the hunter, is fighting for dominance.

I clear my throat and tense my body, mentally shoving Ull down deeper. *Never again*, I think. *I will never be* you *again.*

"Sol," she says, "That's not who the Nephilim are."

I look at her like she's crazy. Of course that's who they are. Ninnis told me.

Ninnis is a liar!

Ninnis is your friend.

"No," I say aloud.

She takes my shoulders. "I don't know all the details, only what Merrill has told me. Which is actually quite a lot. But I'm not an expert."

Merrill. Merrill is my friend. Merrill can be trusted.

NO!

Listen to her.

I clench my eyes shut, willing the voice of Ull to shut up.

I am Solomon. I am Solomon.

"The Sumerians believed they were gods. That much is true. And they record that the Nephilim were also referred to as the Elohim and Anunnaki, both of which mean: those who from Heaven to Earth came."

"Heaven?"

She gives a quick nod.

I fail to hide my skepticism. I've seen and experienced the un-believable, but Heaven? When I speak, my voice is layered with doubt. "Angels?"

She shakes her head and actually manages a small grin. "No, Sol. Not angels. Angels that come to earth, and make their home here are—"

"Demons," I say. This word rings true. There is nothing hea-venly or angelic about my mast—the Nephilim. They are, in every way, demonic. But are they really demons? Fallen angels? I still don't think so. "The Nephilim aren't demons."

"You're right," she says. "They are the *children* of demons. The heroes of old. The men of renown. There is more to that quote, you know. 'The Nephilim were on the earth in those days—and also afterward—when the sons of God (demons) went to the daughters of men (human women) and had children by them. They were the heroes of old, men of renown.' There are several more references to them in the Bible, but that's just one ancient text. There are records of the Nephilim in every ancient culture on Earth. Stories of giants with red hair—"

She takes my hair in her hand and holds it out for me to see. The blood red color makes me sick. I can now remember my real hair, so blond it was almost white. Like Andy Warhol.

"—half human, half animals, double rows of teeth, horns, and strange means of transportation. There are carvings of them all around the world created by cultures separated by thousands of miles and uncrossable oceans. The Nephilim once ruled over mankind, Sol."

"Then what happened?"

"A flood."

"*The* flood?" My skepticism is brewing again. "Like in the Bible?"

She nods. "But not just the Bible. The Sumerians divided time into two Epochs."

"Like B.C. and A.D.?"

She nods. "But for the Sumerians, it was before the flood, and after the flood."

"Then Noah was a Sumerian?"

She shrugs. "In the beginning, I think we all were. But the point is, every ancient text preserved from every ancient culture in the world features the Nephilim, or giants resembling them. A great flood. And the freeing of man from the Nephilim corruption." She pauses, looking unsure of her next words, but speaks them anyway. "Which you have felt first hand."

She's right about that, at least.

"Solomon, the Nephilim are corruptors of mankind, not just

our minds and bodies, but our souls as well. They are our oldest enemy."

The truth of it all settles in. They are, in fact, planning to attack the surface. And I am part of that plan. I am the key. "They're going to make me their leader," I say. "I'm supposed to lead them in a war against humanity."

Her eyes pop open. "When?"

"I don't know. They don't seem to be in a hurry, but within my lifetime."

"Why you?" she asks. "You're...human."

"I'm special," I say. "Merrill told you about what he saw the day I was born?"

"Yes, but—"

"It's all true," I say, and then explain about the spirit of the Nephilim, about how it resides in the land of Antarctica and how it bonded me with the continent when I was born.

"That doesn't sound possible."

"You have no problem with demons mating with humans and a worldwide flood," I say.

She's silent for a moment. "But how did it make you different?"

I close my eyes and focus on the air in the room. I can feel it around me, billions of microscopic molecules. I turn it in my mind. I spin it. When I feel the pull on my hair, I open my eyes. Aimee's rags are waving in the wind. Her braid hovers over her shoulder, held out horizontally. She steps closer to me, into the eye of the small cyclone I have made.

"Okay," she whispers. Terrified.

The wind falls away fast as I feel horrible for scaring her. But she believes me now. "I'm connected to the continent. I feel no cold. The wind, snow, water and land are part of me. I don't know how it works. And *they* don't know about it. I don't think it was supposed to happen."

"Then it's a blessing," she says. "A gift."

"For what?"

"To fight them."

"Fight them?"

She leans in close. "They will enslave the human race if they can, Solomon. They will corrupt us all. They have to be stopped."

All I want to do is take Aimee and leave. I know this is probably impossible now, but I have to try to find a way. We can return to the surface and hop on a plane back to New Hampshire. Back to my parents. And Justin. Mira and Dr. Clark. And forget all about this place. But fight them?

I can't. "If I stay here... They want to— I'm supposed to—"

She takes my hands in hers. "It's okay, Sol. We can figure this out together. You're not alone anymore."

"To become their leader, I need to offer myself...I need to take in the spirit of Nephil."

"The spirit of the Nephilim? You said that happened when you were born."

"Spirit is the word they use for supernatural energy. Like magic. That's what I absorbed when I was born. In this case, it's more of a traditional meaning. The spirit of Nephil, their leader. He was the first Nephilim. The first child born of a human woman and a demon father, if that's what you believe. If I accept his spirit, which is trapped in Tartarus, far below us, it will live in me. I will become him and he me. Being born here, with the Nephilim magic in me, makes me strong enough to contain him, permanently."

"Tartarus?"

"It's a place worse than—"

"I know what Tartarus is, but I never imagined it was—"

"Real?"

She nods.

"I've been thinking the same thing every day since I got here."

A smile stretches onto her face. "I'm sure you have." The smile fades. "If everything you've told me is true, we can't let it happen. We have to stop them."

"Just the two of us?" I laugh at the insanity of it.

"No," she says. "Just you."

My smile fades. She's serious.

"I'm not sure I'll survive the day. I don't know what they have planned for me, do you?"

I don't, and I shake my head. "I won't let them kill you."

"You may not have a choice."

"Why?" I say, my voice raising an octave. "Why do I have to do this?"

"It's not fair," she says. "Lord knows, it's not fair. Your heart...your heart was so pure." She looks at the floor as sadness sweeps over her face. She doesn't want to say any of this to me. But she does, because she believes it. "Sometimes people are chosen for things that are so much bigger than them. But they are given the strength to persevere, to see it through."

"But what can I do?"

"I don't know." Her honesty is killing me. "But you are the next step in their plan. They cannot move forward without you. And that gives you the advantage. No human child has been born on Antarctica since you. You are unique, Sol."

"You think they won't kill me?"

"What do you think?"

I've passed their tests. And I am the only human Antarctican. But can they wait for another? They've waited thousands of years to find me. But in another thousand years, where will the human race be? Probably living on other planets. Probably strong enough to resist them. She's right. If they're going to attack and win, it will have to be soon. With me as Nephil's vessel. "You're right. They won't kill me. But maybe I should kill myself."

She grabs my arm, squeezing tight. For the briefest of moments I have the urge to swat her away, but I fight it. I'm in control. Not Ull.

"Killing yourself is never an option," she says. "You don't think that ever again."

When I don't respond, she takes my chin and gives me a good motherly stare. It feels good to be so cared about. "Never again," she says.

I concede. "Never again. But what then?"

A voice from the hallway makes my hair stand on end. It's Ninnis. He's calling for me. For Ull.

"You're the smartest boy I know, Solomon," she whispers quickly. "You can control the very elements around you. You know what they want. You'll figure out how to stop it."

"I don't think I ca—"

Ninnis calls out again. He's closer now. Approaching the door.

Aimee's eyes widen with fear. "Your face," she says.

I've been crying. My eyes are probably swollen. I can feel my dried tears on my cheeks. Ninnis will see my weakness the moment he opens the door. "Get on the floor. Don't move until we leave."

She listens and immediately dives to the floor, feigning unconsciousness. I jump over her, place Whipsnap next to me and plunge my hands into the bowl of water left for Aimee on a stone countertop. As the door opens I splash the water onto my face and scrub the tears away.

"Ull?" Ninnis says. "What are you doing?"

I turn to Ninnis, fighting a rising sense of doom, and smile. "She threw sand in my eyes." I laugh.

Ninnis approaches and looks at Aimee's motionless form, then to Whipsnap. "You struck her?"

Be Ull, I say to myself. *Adopt his personality, for now.*

"She deserved far more," I say and then point to my vomit. "Once in the stomach to make her bow. A second to her head to silence her."

Ninnis checks her pulse. "She's alive."

"Why?" I ask. "Why is she still alive?"

Ninnis smiles and looks up at my face, which is still dripping with water. "She's to be a teacher." He inspects my eyes. "She got you good."

I rub my eyes. "Does it look that bad?"

"The redness will fade," he says. "You'll look yourself again for the banquet. Of course, we'll have to keep this to ourselves, Ull the future Lord of the Nephilim almost bested by a human woman!" He lets out a guffaw that tenses my back.

I force a laugh of my own. "Let me help break her."

"Alas," he says, "Teachers are not broken. Her knowledge of the outside world is important. Her memories must remain intact, for now. I'm sure when they're done with her, you can do whatever pleases you. Until then, she is not to be harmed." He hands me Whipsnap. "Understood?"

I attach the weapon to my belt, as comfortable with it in my hands as ever. The personality of Ull may be suppressed, but my acquired skills and knowledge have remained. I nod.

"Good," he says. "It's time to go. There are many who want to meet you before we dine. Your reputation has spread to the coasts and beyond."

Beyond? I think, but before I can ask what he means, I see movement outside the door.

35

"Ahh," Ninnis says to the newcomer. "You made it." It's a woman, dressed in clothing similar to mine, but with a breastplate. The weapon hanging from her belt is a mallet with a stone head. One good whack from that could crush just about any skull in the underworld, except maybe a Nephilim's. Her hair is red, like Ninnis's (and mine), but her skin is deeply tan. She is far younger than Ninnis, but she's an adult. I place her around thirty years old, but with time so different down here, she could be eighty. I'm shocked when Ninnis greets her with a hug.

He motions for me to follow him outside Aimee's room, which I now realize is not locked because there is no chance of escape. I leave the room and close the door behind me. Pretending to be Ull will be easier if I know Aimee cannot hear the things I say.

"Ull," Ninnis says, "I'd like you to meet Kainda."

She takes my hand in a crushing grip. For a moment I nearly shout in pain, but then remember who I'm supposed to be. I return the squeeze and then some. My emotions may have returned to a more fragile state, but my body is still strong. I apply pressure until I see her wince. That's when I see the resemblance.

"Your daughter?" I say.

Ninnis looks surprised. "How did you know?"

"You have the same eyes." I work hard to hide my disturbing thoughts but can't resist asking. "She was born here? On Antarctica?"

"I was," she says, "but I'm not like you."

I raise an eyebrow, allowing it to ask the question I can't, because I fear my voice will quiver.

"The breeders have tried to bind humans to the spirit of Antarctica for longer than we have lived," Ninnis says. "They have grown humans. They have bound humans to animals. They have even allowed us hunters to take wives and have children of our own. But nothing has worked. Not until you were born."

"And we had nothing to do with that," Kainda says and then smiles. She is much more pleasant to look at than Ninnis. Her teeth have yet to rot. "You're special."

An honest smile comes to my mouth. "So I've been told."

"And please don't say it again," Ninnis says. "It's going to his head."

The friendly banter is confusing me. Ninnis seems like the polite English gentleman he would have been before his corruption.

Maybe it's Kainda, or simply that my trials have finished. Are the Nephilim more civilized than I have come to believe? Will pretending to be Ull be as hard as I thought?

"If you'd like," Ninnis says, "You may have Kainda as your wife."

My heart hammers in my chest. This will be even harder.

Kainda bows. "It would be my honor."

Ninnis stares at me a moment and then breaks out laughing. "Our fearless hunter is blushing." He claps me hard on the shoulder. "If Kainda is not to your liking, there are many more women for you to choose from. Perhaps even some your age."

Kainda looks positively scorned as Ninnis leads me away. I turn back and offer a, "Nice meeting you." She doesn't reply. She just clips and unclips the hammer hanging next to her slender thigh.

She is beautiful, I think. *In an Amazonian headhunter kind of way.*

"Will she be angry?" I ask once we're out of earshot.

Ninnis cackles. "She has killed for lesser offenses. But she wouldn't dare touch you, lest she be sent to Tartarus herself. And you may yet change your mind about her. She is one of your clan, after all, and clan marriages are preferred."

My mind runs through a list of Norse gods. The hammer is the giveaway. "She belongs to Thor."

"Your observations serve you as well as ever," he says. "Thor is Ull's father. The hierarchy of the clan would normally allow Kainda to choose *you* as her mate. But your future as Nephil's spirit holder gives you...special privileges."

Like the privilege to not have a mate at all, I think. *Not for a long time. And certainly not down here.*

He leads me down a large spiraling staircase. The inner steps are small, human sized. The outer rim has four-foot steps built for Nephilim feet.

At the bottom of the stairs is a creature I've never seen before. It's about five feet tall and spindly, sporting arms and legs like a walking stick insect. But its head is large and shaped like an upside down egg. Two dark almond-shaped eyes frame a tiny nose and a slit for a mouth. It just stands there, watching us.

"Ull, this is Lagash," Ninnis says to me.

"Greetings Ull," I hear, but not with my ears. The voice is in my head.

In my head! Can it hear my thoughts?

I fight my growing panic and say, "Greetings to you, Lagash. You are—"

"A gatherer." Its voice enters my consciousness like a hammer-driven nail. "Do not resist my voice, Ull, it can damage your mind."

I try responding with mine, the way Ull might. *You have not yet known damage.* I focus on an image of me beating Lagash with Whipsnap. *Stay out of my head.*

I see his black eyes shift to my belt. Then he bows and steps away.

A few moments after we pass, Ninnis looks back at Lagash, who is still standing by the stairway. "What did you say to him?"

"I showed him what would happen if he forced his way into my thoughts again."

Ninnis laughs. "Be glad he is a lesser gatherer. The elders are more dangerous than any warrior."

"Be sure to point them out to me, then, so that I do not offend." I fake a laugh and give Ninnis a punch in the shoulder the way Justin used to do to me, the way that says, *we're friends.*

We're in a part of the citadel I've never seen before. The hallway is lined by massive, forty foot doors. Ancient statues fill house-sized alcoves. And carvings, as detailed as those found in the world's ancient tombs, decorate the walls. I can hear voices and footsteps beyond the doors. But we see no one else. He leads me to a set of double doors so vast I think you could fit a 747 through them.

He shouts out in a language I don't understand, then notes my attention. "Sumerian," he says. "The original language of the Nephilim, which was then taught to men. You'll learn it soon enough."

A loud creaking echoes in the vast hall as the doors open inward.

On the other side is a space built like, and as large as, a football stadium. A staircase descends to the floor, perhaps fifty feet below. Lining the edges of the space are skins and furs arranged into human and Nephilim sized lounging areas. Spread throughout are creatures cooking on spits. Bowls of food I don't recognize are arranged around the rooms. And the smell, even to my newfound self, makes my stomach rumble. I may no longer be Ull anymore, but I am still accustomed to the food here. And it has been some time since I ate.

But the creaking of the door has captured the attention of the fifty-odd creatures in the room. There are ten Nephilim warriors, some wearing masks I recognize as the heads of more famous gods: Anubis, Zeus, Odin and others. Ull is there, too. There are a few gatherers staring up at me with their big black eyes, but I don't feel them in my head. There are bulbous sickly looking things with rolls of fat that cascade like waves when they move. Their round faces are feminine, but few other features are apparent. Even their arms seem to have been overtaken and absorbed by their fat. There is a group of humans, dressed for some ancient battle. These are my fellow hunters. When I see Kainda standing among them already, I make a mental note that she is fast. I see others in a flash. Strange creatures, some of which appear to be half man, half animal, but I don't have time to get a good look.

One of the warriors has stood. His hair is red, like the rest, but his eyes are yellow. When I see the dark leather garb that matches that of Ninnis, I know who he is: Enki, first son of Nephil.

When his eyes meet mine, even across a distance of more than one hundred feet, I have to fight to not show my revulsion. But the stare is short lived. He bares his teeth in a snarl, turns his head to the ceiling two hundred feet above and lets out a howl. Soon everyone in the room is howling, even Ninnis.

For a moment, I'm dumbfounded. What's going on? Then I realize this is their applause. They are praising me. I feel a swell of pride as the intensity of the sound shakes me to the core.

Then I'm howling with them.

A smile creeps onto my face.

Ull is rising.

36

Energy courses through my body. I feel bonded to all in the room. The howl, just now ending, creates a strong sense of belonging to the pack. Like wolves. A tingle rolls down my spine and my hair stands on end. And when the chamber has fallen silent again, I stand in awe of what I have just experienced. When the energy fades, so does Ull, and that awe is replaced by repulsion. But that dark side of me arrived at an opportune time. When Ninnis claps me on the shoulder, I know joining in was the right thing to do.

Enki bows his head slightly and opens his arms, motioning to the room as if to say, this is all for you. Then he sits and begins to eat once more. The menagerie of Nephilim follows his cue, and the feast begins anew.

I am thankful for this. There will be no speeches. No idle chitchat. This is a time of primal bonding.

I follow Ninnis down the staircase and into the stadium-sized lower floor. The first creatures to greet me look like gatherers, but are covered in green scaly skin, almost like a cresty's, and have yellow eyes, like Enki's. The things ooze malevolence, but they bow as we pass.

"The seekers," Ninnis says to me. "They work closely with, but do not always get along with, the gatherers. They have been subservient to the gatherers since their coup failed."

This news astonishes me. I pictured the Nephilim as one big happy—yet exceedingly evil—family, bound to a common goal. Ninnis senses my question. "The Nephilim have warred among themselves for centuries, culling the weak as they do."

"Have the hunters ever revolted?" I ask.

"We are not fully Nephilim. It is not our right," he says, and I think, *revolution is never a right, but is always an option.* I stay silent though, because he continues, "...though we may take part in battle if commanded by our masters."

"Aren't all the Nephilim our masters?"

"No. Ull is your master. Enki is mine."

"What happens if one of our masters dies?"

Ninnis looks at me with a raised eyebrow. "Such a thing hasn't happened since the death of Nephil. Killing warriors is near impossible, but it's also forbidden. They are the strongest. And will lead the battle against the topside. By your side, of course."

I make an effort to puff up my chest with pride, but I'm really just trying to keep myself from passing out. "You didn't answer my question."

"Without a master," Ninnis says. "You would be free."

A genuine smile fights to spread my lips. I resist it, but the twitch in my facial expression hasn't gone unnoticed. "You find that pleasing?"

"Not at all," I say. "I will be free soon enough."

He turns fully toward me, confusion and anger tensing his forehead into a maze of crisscrossing lines. In that moment I am reminded of how old Ninnis is, despite his physical ability. "When I accept the spirit of Nephil," I add. "I will have no mas-ter."

Ninnis pauses. And then laughs. "Right you are!"

When we reach the bottom of the stairs, I feel positively puny, like I've been shrunk down to the size of an ant. The ceiling is so far above me. Even the smallest of the Nephilim, the gatherers, stand taller than me. And the tallest, Enki and the other warriors, tower over me, even when they're sitting on the floor.

But all of them bow. Every single one, until we reach the fat one.

She (I call her a she because her eyes are vaguely feminine) is revolting. From a distance, I could not see the details of this thing. Where a nose and mouth should be, there is something that looks more like a beak. And indeed, there are feathers on her head instead of hair. The body is composed of rolls of fat that have enveloped her arms and legs almost completely. I think I see wiggling fingers protruding from a spot half way up, but it's im-possible to tell. She could just as easily have stubby wings. Her head sits atop the mass of flesh like a cherry on a fifteen foot tall ice cream sundae.

"She does not bow," I observe.

"Breeders are unable to move," he says, pointing to what looks like a massive stretcher beneath her body. "They cannot move without assistance and only the warriors are strong enough to move them. Gaia is here because she was your breeder."

This last statement stuns me twice. The first is the revelation that this sickly blobbish bird-woman-thing is Gaia, the Greek fertility goddess otherwise known as Mother Earth. She's depicted so beautifully in the books I've read. The second is that she is somehow associated with me. "*My* breeder?"

"Where do you think all the feeders came from?"

"Feeders?"

Ninnis chuckles. "That's right. You call them egg-monsters. She was far above you in the pit. She could not see you, but she could hear you, and smell you. The feeders hatch from her eggs."

This is far beyond anything I'd expected. I scan the room quickly and see several roast feeders on spits. "They're Nephilim? They eat their own young? *I* ate their young?"

"It is the purpose for which they are born," Ninnis says. "True Nephilim are born of human mothers, not Nephilim mothers."

I can feel my stomach tensing and keep talking to distract myself. "What happens if they are not eaten? Do they die?"

"If a feeder escapes into the wild and survives, they become insatiable eating machines larger than any Nephilim." He glances at me. "May you never run into one."

My eyebrows rise. "There are loose feeders?"

"Three," he says. "They roam the largest, deepest tunnels underground, eating everything that crosses their path."

With a shake of my head, I look back at Gaia. "What do the breeders eat, if they can't move?"

He stops. "Watch. It shouldn't take long. They're always eating."

We stand there for a moment. Then I see a centipede crawl out of a crack in the wall behind the breeder. It crawls up her feathered backside and scrambles toward the head.

"Is she emitting a pheromone?" I ask.

"A what?"

I have to remind myself that Ninnis's education is a hundred years old, and I would guess didn't include much science to begin with. "It's like a scent. Something that attracts the centipede."

He nods. "I think so."

The centipede stands beneath Gaia's open beak and rises up, its antennae twitching. With a snap, the beak closes down over the creature, consuming half of it with one bite. She tilts her head back while the centipede's legs twitch madly. With a flex of her throat, the centipede vanishes.

I turn away. To watch any more is to invite intestinal doom.

I see several more different variants of Nephilim, but I never get a chance to ask about them. We have arrived at our destination. A group of ten hunters lounge on the floor, all sharing a roast feeder and cups of water. All are dressed formally in leathers and carry a variety of weapons—swords, knives, hammers, maces, bows and arrows—but nothing quite as unique, or homemade, as Whipsnap and my climbing claws.

Kainda glares at me for a moment, then tears a chunk of flesh from the feeder and gnaws on it. The rest bow and move their limbs to allow Ninnis and I passage to what I assume is my spot. As far as I can tell, it is the only seat in the room, and looks like a throne cut from solid stone. I sit in its fur-covered seat and find it quite comfortable, almost like it can hide me from the monsters surrounding me.

Ninnis sits on the floor next to me.

"Why am I in a chair?" I ask, "While everyone else sits on the floor?"

"This does not please you?"

His question makes me remember that it *should* please me. I am Ull! I laugh. "It pleases me very much. I was wondering what the significance was."

"It represents your future throne," Ninnis says. "After the bonding."

I see another glare from Kainda shot in my direction, and something inside me snaps. Perhaps it's a little bit of Ull, I don't know. But when she takes another chunk of flesh from the feeder, I take hold of Whipsnap, pull it free and send its blade snapping into the meat, pulling it from her hand.

The other hunters fall silent. I bring the meat to my mouth and take a bite. When I'm done, all but one of the hunters is grinning. Kainda is not. So I fix her with a stare of my own and say, "Rude not to offer your future lord something to eat."

All eyes turn to Kainda and she is forced to bow.

"You are bold beyond wisdom," Ninnis whispers to me.

He's right, of course. I can't say what got into me. Ull is my only excuse, but I can't say that. To Ninnis, I *am* Ull.

Before I can respond, a booming voice fills the chamber. It is Enki. He's speaking Sumerian so I can't understand what he's saying, but there is a howl in response to it. The howl brings a surge of energy, but I don't join in this time.

Neither does Kainda.

Enki walks toward the hunters. He could squash every last one of us in just a few stomps of his massive foot. But he kneels down on one knee, offers a bow and holds out a glass vial that looks tiny in his hand. "It is time, little Ull, to accept your place among us."

Enki glances at Ninnis and communicates something with his eyes. Ninnis hops to his feet and takes the vial from Enki. He approaches me, holding the now small container like it is a holy relic.

I realize that's precisely what it is when Enki speaks again. "This flask holds the last drops of blood from our lord, Nephil. It is the last of his body left on this Earth, free from the confines of Tartarus."

A howl follows this statement.

"With his blood, you will bind your body with his." He's speaks directly to me now. "Over time, it will make you stronger and prepare you for the spirit of Nephil. This is a privilege beyond description and an honor we can only bestow once. Are you prepared to accept the body of Nephil? Are you willing to surrender yourself to his spirit? Will you, as lord Nephil, lead his children against the human race?" This last part is said loudly, with arms outstretched, and it is met with the loudest howl of the night.

I can feel Ull clawing to get out, but I resist him. I need to make this decision, not him, and every atom in my body is screaming, *NO!* It will mean revealing I am no longer Ull the hunter. It will mean my death.

Not your death, a voice inside me says. Ull?

They will not kill you.

They will break you.

Again.

Say, no.

His agreement with my decision to decline reveals the error of my ways.

No, no, no.

It takes all my effort, but I speak my one word reply with a grin.

Say, NO!

"Yes."

37

Ninnis slowly raises the vial toward me. I detect a slight shake in his hands. His eyes are glued, not on me, his future lord, but on the blood. There is an undeniable craving in his eyes.

In *all* the hunters' eyes.

I suspect many of them are fighting the urge to take the blood for themselves. Perhaps this was an honor for which all of them were considered? Perhaps they're just envious?

Whatever the cause, something is holding them back. They'd have to get through Ninnis first, who despite craving the liquid himself, is unshakably loyal to the Nephilim. I would come next, striking with Whipsnap (well, Ull would, I'm not entirely sure what I would do) and perhaps even Enki would get involved. But even then, if they survived all of that and drank the blood, would they survive the physical bonding with Nephil's body?

I suspect not. And I think that is the most likely reason none of them acts on their desire.

The vial is warm to the touch, as though the blood has just been drawn. I think about drinking the ancient liquid and become queasy.

Can I do this?

I look around seeing hundreds of eyes turned toward me, some of them larger than my head. I know there's no choice. I must do this.

To survive.

For Aimee.

For everyone I love on the surface, who will die if the Nephilim invade.

I pull the stopper and hold the vial in the air, instigating a howl that I hope will supply me with courage. As the howl reverberates through the chamber and my body, I place the vial to my lips and turn it up. But the liquid does not immediately fall. Despite being part supernatural, the blood has dried some. It slides down the throat of the vial slowly, a gelatinous blob.

The blood falls into my mouth and I immediately know the squishy mass is too big and too solid to swallow hole. With my eyes closed and my head still turned toward the ceiling, I give Nephil's blood three solid chews and then swallow.

I can feel it, sliding down my throat, but there is no other change aside from the tears of disgust building in my eyes.

Then it hits my stomach with the force of a giant's fist. I pitch forward, screaming in pain. A burning flows through my veins, moving down my legs and then back up. My torso is next, then my neck and finally my brain. The burning speeds my thoughts and heightens my awareness. But I am still me. Nephil's body has no effect on my thoughts.

And I can only think of one thing as I curl into a ball, gritting my teeth and wailing with pain: run!

Now is the time. I am the carrier of Nephil's blood. They cannot kill me. With it, I may be strong enough to resist breaking if I'm captured. I may be strong enough to undo everything they have spent thousands of years preparing for. But I must run.

Now.

I focus this burning energy far beyond myself, reaching out to something beyond my intellect. The burning in my veins is matched by a strong wind now roaring through the underground tunnels. The snapping of my over-tense muscles is mirrored by the cracking of the continent's stratus layer as water finds a new path.

My only chance of escape is chaos.

And to do that I must give the Nephilim something they have never seen before. Something they do not enjoy. Something they fear.

I hear Ninnis speaking to me. I cannot hear his words, but I detect concern. Was I supposed to experience this pain? Did any of them know what, if anything, would happen when I drank the blood? As the pain subsides, a grin replaces my gritted teeth. They fear they have chosen wrong. That I am not strong enough to contain the essence of Nephil.

Assuaging their fears, I uncurl and stand. Something about me must look different, because they stare at me with wide eyes. Even Enki looks stunned. But I am not concerned with what they think. My energy is focused above them.

It's only a few seconds before someone notices and shouts out in Sumerian. All heads turn up. Including mine.

Swirling at the top of the chamber is a black cloud. It's small, but it quickly grows in size as water pours in from above. When the cloud fills the upper atmosphere of the chamber, the temperature suddenly drops.

I hear Enki growl. He's not enjoying this. But he also doesn't know if this was caused by my bonding with Nephil. In fact, he may be wondering if it's Nephil doing this.

The warm air at the bottom of the chamber mixes with the cold air above. The friction builds quickly. A blinding light flashes across the ceiling accompanied by a crack of thunder so loud even the seasoned hunters sitting before me cup their ears.

Then, miles underground, where the temperature is a steady sixty-five degrees and weather doesn't exist, it snows. And not gently. The whiteout is as intense as anything ever seen on the surface. And the wind whips around the chamber like a cyclone.

Everyone is blind.

Except for me.

The wind parts the snow for me, creating a path to the stairs and then to the massive doors above, which have blown open. I run to the stairs and take them two at a time, shedding my armor and cloak as I go. Where I'm headed, it will only slow me down. I leave on my leather undergarments and the belt which holds my weapons, everything else remains on the stairs.

I enter the tunnel beyond the exit and find it empty. There are a hundred ways to flee from here, many better than the one I choose, but I must see Aimee before I leave. I find the spiral staircase and charge up.

The storm has ended. I can feel it. If not for the energy provided by Nephil's blood, I would have never been able to pull the storm together this far underground. Even now, I can feel my energy falling back to normal levels. I'm just thankful the storm didn't exhaust me, like it did on the surface when I took Aimee.

But even at full strength, I may not be able to escape. Once they recover from the storm and find me missing, the search will begin. I need to be gone from this place when that happens.

At last I can see Aimee's room ahead. I sprint for the door and open it without knocking. She's sitting on the bed. Her head snaps up, and for a moment she smiles. Then she sees the look of panic on my face.

She stands. "What happened?"

"I need to go," I say. "But I needed to thank you first."

"For what?"

"For saving me. For forgiving me despite the awful things I did to you. I'm not sure how you can."

"Solomon," she says with a slight smile. "Nothing is unforgivable. And it was not you who did those things."

I embrace her hard and then step back. "I might be gone for a while, but someday, we'll both leave this place. I promise."

She squeezes my hand and says, "We'll leave together," but I can see the doubt in her eyes. "Go," she says. "And don't worry about me. I'll be fine."

My look of doubt is impossible to hide, too.

"Just like living in a lion's den," she says.

I have no idea what she's talking about, but her smile is genuine. I step back into the hallway and am stopped in my tracks by a booming voice that sounds more confused than angry. "What are you doing?"

It's Ull. He's not wet from the snow. I hadn't seen him leave the banquet hall, but he must have. And now he's seen me with Aimee.

Far from being stupid, Ull puts the pieces together quickly. I'm no longer dressed for the feast. I'm saying goodbye to the human I captured. And I'm terrified by his presence.

I think it's my fear that tips him off. He sees the change in me. Knows I'm me again.

But I'm not as weak as he thinks. I may not be a savage killer, but I will defend the people I care about. And if Ull lives, Aimee will surely die or be tortured. And I will not allow that to happen.

I step out into the middle of the hall and face my master. With one hand on Whipsnap, I look him in the eyes, pour on an English accent and repeat the quote I used in the arena, which I now remember comes from *Oliver.* "Please, sir, may I have some more?"

I have no doubt he remembers the odd phrase composed of the last rebellious words I spoke before he broke me, body and mind, endearing my will to his.

His response is immediate.

And violent.

His axe cuts through the air so fast I barely have time to respond. I leap up and the axe passes below me, so close that I actually roll off of its blade and back to my feet. I know what's coming next, so I'm already focusing on creating a strong wind. Three arrows, each a kill shot, are deflected away from me at the last moment. Two slam into the far wall and stick. The third ricochets off.

Losing his patience, Ull tosses the bow to the side, most likely recalling he had to get up close and personal in our first encounter. I remember it too, and decide I would prefer to stay out of his reach. I need to reach his head, remove that golden crown and see how well that protected part of the warrior body heals. But there are no god-heads carved into the stone and I don't have my rope.

Still, there might be another way. Not all of the energy delivered by Nephil has left. I still have some strength. And if I can deflect massive arrows...

I take Whipsnap from my belt. It springs to life in my hand, like a living thing, eager once more for the hunt. But this is no hunt. It's a fight.

To the death.

I charge, bending Whipsnap in my hands. Ull charges too. His arm is raised back, ready to smash me to the floor like a fly. One good hit, that's all it will take, and this will be over.

Whether it's him striking me, or me him. Either way, one of us is going to die.

Twenty feet away he begins to swing.

I jump.

For a moment I can see his swing is going to connect. Then the wind picks me up and carries me higher. His eyes go wide with the realization that he has missed. This tiny insect can fly, albeit briefly.

He tries to duck to the side, but Whipsnap has a good reach and when I let it loose, it connects with the crown as it did in the arena. And just like then, the crown flies from his head. I think, *what a fool* (for not securing it tighter) and then concentrate my energy far behind me, far down the hallway where one of Ull's arrows lies on the floor.

Everything moves slowly. The crown is still sailing away, flipping end over end like a tossed coin. Ull's forehead is exposed. The loose skin pulses with his heartbeat. I can hear it. Thum. Thum. Thum. I focus on it. Even as I fall, I will the wind toward it.

The arrow passes over me in a blur, moving as fast as it did from Ull's bow. But this time, the projectile finds its target. I hear a tearing sound followed by a *slurp*. The impact knocks the giant off his feet. He falls beneath me.

I land on Ull's still chest. The arrow is buried in his forehead. And he doesn't move. The giant is dead.

The Nephilim *can* be killed.

I stand up, looking down at my former master and realize I am free. Not from pursuit, or threat of life, slavery or future breaking. But free of the monster I called my master. A part of me loved this thing, the way an abused person loves an abuser, but my eyes have been opened.

"I am free," I say, and a single set of ears hears me.

I turn and face Ninnis, who has just reached the top of the staircase. He's soaking wet and has a funny look on his face. I realize it's because I'm standing on the chest of a dead Nephilim. "They can be killed," I say to him.

His face is grim. Unreadable. He shakes his head, and then runs away.

Though this is out of character for Ninnis, I know not to waste time questioning it. My retreat takes me in an opposite direction, and I find the path wonderfully free of pursuers.

* * *

I squeeze through a maze of passageways, covering my tracks as best I can. I travel in water whenever possible to erase my scent. I move for days without stopping for food.

Despite my hunger, every step away from Asgard fills me with a hopeful energy. Even in the darkness, there can be light. My mind returns to that day in the car. We're on the way to Logan airport. Mira is sitting next to me. The photo of us is in my hand. And *Open Up Your Heart (And Let the Light Shine In)* by Gail & Rosemary Clooney is playing on the oldies station. Mira knows it and sings along.

Mommy told me something a little girl should know
It's all about the Devil and I've learned to hate him so
She says he causes trouble when you let him in the room

He will never ever leave you if your heart is filled with gloom

So, let the sun shine in, face it with a grin
Smilers never lose and frowners never win
So, let the sun shine in, face it with a grin
Open up your heart and let the sun shine in

The memory is infectious and the lyrics reflect how I feel. I play it back in my head, and I'm soon singing along quietly. I'm whistling the song, feeling hopeful about the future and eventually rescuing Aimee, but when I reach my destination, Ninnis is waiting for me.

38

"Nice tune," he says, leaning against the tunnel wall. He looks calm, collected and refreshed.

"How did you find me?" I ask, my hand resting on Whipsnap.

"If you're wondering how I tracked you, I didn't. You covered your scent nicely. But I knew where you were going."

I squint at him, asking *how* without saying a word.

"Where is it?" he asks. "Where did you hide it?"

I stay silent. I answer only to myself now.

"I knew you couldn't destroy it."

"Why didn't you say anything about it?"

He smiles. "We all keep trinkets from the topside. You were doing so well I didn't see the harm in it."

"Whoops," I say.

"Was it the photo?" he asks. "Is that what brought your memories back? They *are* back?"

I nod. There's no reason to lie about that. "Not the photo."

I shrug. "I think it was Nephil's blood." Now *this* I need to lie about. To protect Aimee. "Must have made my mind strong enough to undo the breaking."

He ponders this before offering his own shrug. "You won't come back?"

"What about Ull?"

"Without a witness they won't know if you killed him or if you had help, which it certainly appears you did, though you and I both know that's not true."

"You weren't witness?" I ask.

"A witness who also happened to be your trainer. When you killed Ull you put my reputation in jeopardy. I would be strung up, filleted alive and fed to a breeder if they knew the truth."

"What do they know?"

"That something strange happened when you were bonded with the blood of Nephil. That you disappeared shortly after. And that someone, most likely another warrior, killed Ull."

Which means, I think, *with the exception of Ninnis, my escape has gone perfectly.* "When I stood up after taking the blood. Before the storm. What was everyone looking at?"

"You haven't seen it?"

I shake my head. I have no idea what he's talking about.

He motions to his head. "Your hair. There's a streak in it."

A streak? I'm fairly certain the coloring of my hair over time represented the progress of my corruption. I was fairly certain the change was permanent. "What color?" I ask.

"Blond," he says.

I want to smile. To leap with joy. Maybe everything that's been done to me can be undone or repaired? Maybe one day I'll see the sky and not need to squint. Or I'll share a birthday meal with friends. Or any number of things I took for granted before. But in my heart, I know those things are a long way off. "What happens now?"

He shifts away from the wall, casually holding his hands behind his back. "All of the hunters have been sent out to search for you. They will track you down, subdue you if necessary, and bring you back."

"But that's not why you're here," I say, looking back down the tunnel. "You came alone."

He grins. "I'm here to break you. Again. And bring back Ull, the hunter."

When he pulls his hand out from behind his back, I give a yank on Whipsnap. My weapon cracks open, but is immediately pulled from my hand. Ninnis knew I would use Whipsnap and snared it with a line, yanking it away. He tosses my weapon behind him.

For a moment, I think he's going to say something again. But he lets out a wail as savage as anything I've ever heard in the underworld or above it, and charges. His arms are outstretched. His fingers curve into hooks.

I fall back under him, unprepared for such ferocity. Ull would have been, but I'm not him anymore.

When I hit the stone floor, Ninnis has my arms pinned back. His long, thick, and sharpened fingernails are digging into my skin.

This is how it starts.

The breaking.

And I can feel a part of me—the part that flinches under Justin's punches or weeps when my mother laughs at me—shirking back. But I'm more than that now. I have been broken and repaired. I have all the skills of a Nephilim hunter. I am bonded with the continent of Antarctica on a supernatural level. I am the killer of warriors and have consumed the blood of Nephil, lord of the Nephilim.

"AND YOU THINK *YOU* CAN BREAK ME?"

The voice is unnatural.

I'm not even sure it was mine. But it came out of my mouth and roared like thunder.

A wind kicks up from the tunnel below and races toward us. Ninnis has let go of me and sat up. He's shaking with fear.

Then an invisible force strikes him and carries him up the steeply graded tunnel. I pick up Whipsnap and give chase, but I lose sight of him when he's launched from the tunnel like a human cannonball.

I enter the night and find a clear sky full of stars and a full moon. It's bright enough to make me squint. Ninnis lies still, three hundred feet below. I go to him and crouch down. His chest rises and falls. He is alive.

I could kill him now. It would be so easy.

Without realizing I'm doing it, I place Whipsnap's blade against his throat. I see myself cutting him open, watching his blood gush into the white snow.

And I remember the voice.

My voice, that was not mine.

The bloodlust reveals that I have more than just Ull inside me now. There is a new voice.

Nephil.

Some part of him is there. Fighting for control.

And I won't give it. Not to either of them.

In all my time underground, I have killed to eat, I have killed in self-defense. Insects. Dinosaurs. Feeders. Dozens of other stranger creatures. Including Nephilim. But I have never killed a human being.

And I'm not going to start now. Not by the direct action of running him through, nor by the indirect action of leaving him to freeze to death.

I take Ninnis by the hand and drag him back to the tunnel entrance. This will be the second time I've spared his life. I doubt he will honor my mercy by returning the favor, but to save myself, I need to save him too.

I leave him sitting by the entrance and scrawl three words into the stone wall across from him. It will be the first thing he sees when he wakes up. I'm not sure the power of the words will affect him as they did me, but I can hope.

Further down the tunnel, I stop by a crack in the wall. It takes me thirty seconds to work the Polaroid photo out of the wall with Whipsnap's blade tip. I risked everything for this photo, heading to familiar territory when I should have been headed deep. But when I look at the image and see my face, so young and so happy, and next to me is Mira—the sight of her breaks my heart—I feel the voices in me fall silent. This photo is my anchor to myself and to everything I'm fighting for.

But right now, I can't fight. I'm not even sure how to fight what is coming. Despite all I can do, I am just one person alone against a supernatural army. So I run. As fast and as deep as I dare, I run.

39

Forty days later, I stop. Though I'm not sure it was really forty days, by underground standards or topside standards. I haven't slept much. But I've traveled far and deep and have found a place I think the Nephilim, and the hunters will at least think twice about before following me.

It's one of the largest caverns I've seen. The ceiling is hundreds of feet up but not concealed in darkness. Instead, it's covered in the luminescent crystals that lined the pit. So many, in fact, that I need a few minutes to adjust to the light.

I stand at the edge of a waterfall, looking down. Below me is a lake, not as vast as the one at New Jericho, but big enough. And the light shines on the water just right, so I can see the animals living in the water. There are fish, lots of them, but none are large enough to eat me. There are no seals here, either. If there were, I imagine the cavern's primary denizen and topper of the food chain—a pack of cresties led by a thirty-foot matriarch—would have eaten them long ago.

Living among cresties is a risk, but there are several other animals living here, and more than a few of them are prey for the cresties. As long as they don't detect my scent, which seemed to have set off the first mother cresty I encountered, I should be fine.

And the risk is worth it. Not only are there fish and other prey animals to eat—birds, both in the air and flightless, what appear to be herds of hairless mammals, and if necessary, the cresties—but there are also plants. Trees, shrubs and vines surround the lake. Plains of tall green grasses roll into the distance. I have no idea how this is possible, without sunlight. Maybe the stones actually produce ultraviolet light? Maybe the spirit of Antarctica makes it possible.

I don't know.

I honestly don't care.

All I know is that I can live here. Maybe long enough to repair my soul. Or come up with a plan.

What I don't know, is how to get down.

I am perched three hundred feet above the lake. The rocks to either side of the river are slick and impossible to climb down. I've already backtracked and searched side tunnels with no luck. Short of spending months exploring miles upon miles of cave systems, this is the only entrance to sanctuary.

Then I remember who I have become.

"I am Solomon," I say. "Solomon Vincent, the first and only child born on Antarctica. I am home."

I walk into the river. Like so many other things in this land that seem to crave my death, the water fights to pull me over the edge. But I've learned to stand against such things. I can stand in the river and walk against its power. I can focus my will upon it and redirect its flow. Maybe even move mountains when I'm strong enough. Or, if I choose, I can go with the flow—

—and jump.

40

When Ninnis woke, he didn't open his eyes. He allowed his other senses to reach out first, showing no signs of consciousness. There was a cold breeze on his skin, but not too cold. He'd been brought back into the tunnel. And though his body ached, he could tell his wayward protégé hadn't beaten him. In fact, it seemed the boy had saved his life by dragging him back inside.

Ninnis could still smell Solomon, but the scent was faint, faded by hours.

He listened but heard nothing more than the distant wind outside.

He was alone.

With his head tilted toward the floor, he opened his eyes. He inspected his toes and remaining fingers. No signs of frostbite.

Why? He thought. *Why didn't he kill me?*

He must know I'll find him again. And if I can't break him, I'll kill him. Better that he disappears forever than stain my reputation with the truth.

But can I kill him?

He repeated the question in his mind, over and over, and never came up with an answer. He was mortal. That was certain. But the true extent of the boy's abilities were unknown.

His affronts against the masters couldn't be overlooked. If he would not serve them, he would die, and the battle against the human race would have to be fought under Enki's rule—something that had been proposed in the past. Only Enki's insistence that they free Nephil had stopped the movement.

But with Nephil's blood consumed by a hunter turned rogue, what was to stop them? The hunt for Solomon would continue, but at some point, whether he was never found or found by Ninnis and killed, the war would have to be waged.

And what could stop them? What force on earth could stand in the way of the mighty Nephilim?

Ninnis looked up and found the answer to his question etched in the stone wall.

I forgive you.

ABOUT THE AUTHOR

JEREMY ROBINSON is the author of ten thrillers including Pulse and Instinct, the first two books in his exciting Jack Sigler series. His novels have been translated into eight languages. He is also the director of New Hampshire AuthorFest, a non-profit organization promoting literacy. He lives in New Hampshire with his wife and three children.

Connect with Robinson online:
Twitter: www.twitter.com/jrobinsonauthor
Myspace: www.myspace.com/sciencethriller
Facebook: www.facebook.com/sciencethriller
Website: www.jeremyrobinsononline.com

COMING SUMMER 2011

PURSUIT

BOOK II OF THE ANTARKTOS SAGA

TO STAY INFORMED VISIT
WWW.JEREMYROBINSONONLINE.COM
AND SIGN UP FOR THE NEWSLETTER

CPSIA information can be obtained at www.ICGtesting.com
227036LV00002B/108/P